CAMPUS FLIRT

JENNIFER SUCEVIC

Campus Flirt

Cover Design by Mary Ruth Baloy at MR Creations

Editing by Evelyn Summers

Home | Jennifer Sucevic or www.jennifersucevic.com

Subscribe to my newsletter -) https://www.subscribepage.com/l5v9e4

ALSO BY JENNIFER SUCEVIC

Campus God

Campus Heartthrob

Campus Hottie

Campus Player

Claiming What's Mine

Confessions of a Heartbreaker

Crazy for You (80s short story)

Don't Leave

Friend Zoned

Hate to Love You

Heartless

If You Were Mine

Just Friends

King of Campus

King of Hawthorne Prep

Love to Hate You

One Night Stand

Protecting What's Mine

Queen of Hawthorne Prep

Stay

The Boy Next Door

The Breakup Plan

The Girl Next Door

SASHA

"Have you given any more consideration to going out with my cousin?" my bestie asks as we trudge across campus to our nine o'clock class.

Of course she would hit me with this when I'm still bleary-eyed from lack of caffeine. I woke up late and didn't have time to make a cup of java before rushing out the door.

When I remain silent, she lifts a brow.

In all honesty, I'd been hoping Brooke would forget about her stint as matchmaker and stop trying to fix me up with her cousin, Ryder. I should have known better. My roommate isn't the type of girl to let anything go. She can be as tenacious as a terrier when the occasion calls for it. It's all part of her charm. She'll nip at my heels until she wears me down and I eventually give in.

Or I kick her in the ass. Whichever comes first.

"Well?" She nudges my shoulder with her own.

I huff out a breath before hedging, "Do you really think that's a good idea?" Because I think it's a terrible one.

"Absolutely. Why wouldn't it be? He's good looking. You're good looking. Voilà! It's a match made in heaven."

The only true part of that statement is that Ryder McAdams is smoking hot. And he has the puck bunnies to prove his popularity. I, however, am not interested in dating a jock. I've spent most of my life around them. Football players, to be specific. My best guy friend—the one I've known since we were in diapers—is a half-back for the Western Wildcats. I've seen firsthand how rabid the fangirls are for him and his teammates. I have zero interest in competing with a legion of jersey chasers in order to hold on to a boyfriend.

And the other downside to dating an athlete is that a lot of these guys aren't known for their fidelity.

Just ask Brooke.

She was dating Andrew—a football player—for about nine months. Little did she know that he had a few groupies on the side and was busy spreading around the love. An unfortunate clap diagnosis is what ultimately tipped her off. Or maybe I should say it was the painful urination and weird vaginal discharge that clued her in to the situation.

Eww.

I'd thought she was going to wring his neck with her bare hands. Honestly, he deserved that and more. Brooke was the best girlfriend. And even though he keeps crawling back on his hands and knees, begging her to give him another chance, my girl has remained steadfast in her resolve. I couldn't be prouder of her. She's told him in no uncertain terms to go take a flying leap. So far, he refuses to take no for an answer. I'm not sure why he won't let it go. He obviously didn't care enough about their relationship to stay faithful in the first place.

So...no, I'd prefer to avoid the athletes at Western.

Along with the frat boys on campus.

They're just as bad.

Take out those two groups of potential candidates and it makes for an awfully shallow dating pool.

"I'm not really looking for a relationship," I tell her as we pass by the union. "I've got enough going on." Soccer and school take up a huge chunk of my time. I'm in my senior year of college and my schedule is jam packed with architecture classes. I'm also working on getting my resume together so I'll have a job secured by the time graduation rolls around in the spring. Life is changing. I'm both excited and scared at the prospect.

"Maybe not, but you need someone to take your mind off Easton. You gotta move on, girl."

The comment is so unexpected that I stumble in surprise. Before I can take out any of the unfortunate pedestrians within striking distance, Brooke grabs hold of my elbow and tows me along the walkway. It takes a moment to regain my balance.

Panic bursts to life inside me as I focus on staying upright. "What are you talking about?"

My roommate rolls her eyes and releases a long-suffering sigh. "I'm talking about the secret crush on E you've got going on." She pulls me closer before dropping the next bomb. "The one, I suspect, you've had for years."

I shake my head in silent protest.

Before I can deny her claims, she continues. "You can try to fool me all you like, but don't lie to yourself. You've had a major thing for that boy as long as I've known you. And hey—it's not like I blame you for it. Easton is gorgeous with all that thick, whiskey-colored hair. There's been more than a few times when I've wanted to drag my fingers through it." A faraway look enters her eyes as she stares off into space before abruptly clearing her throat. "Anyway, the point I'm trying to make is that I get it. My problem with the situation is that you're unwilling to do anything about it. The best thing you could do is move on. And Ryder could help with that. It's not like I'm telling you to marry the dude. I'm just saying, let him take you out and show you a good time."

Even though she's right and I should come clean, I mumble, "I don't have a crush on him. We're just friends. That's it." It's hard to admit the truth—even to yourself—when you've spent years tamping down the emotion and pretending it doesn't exist.

Brooke spears me with a pitying look. "Oh, Sash. That's so sad."

My shoulders collapse under the weight of her disappointment.

Secretly, I can't help but agree. It *is* sad. Pathetic, even.

"Why don't you just tell him how you feel?"

Is she legit crazy?

"And ruin our friendship?" I blurt before I can stop myself. "Hard pass. Plus, he doesn't see me that way." He never has.

"How do you know? Have you ever asked?"

"Of course not," I mutter, desperate to change the subject. "Easton doesn't see me as anything more than a friend. His best friend. And I love having him in my life. I would never do anything to jeopardize our relationship."

Just as she opens her mouth to bombard me with more questions, a muscular arm is thrown over my shoulders and I'm hauled against a hard body. Even before his masculine scent can inundate my senses, I know exactly who I've been crushed against. And yes...it takes every ounce of self-control to resist burrowing against his comforting strength.

That's when I realize Brooke is right. I need to stop lying to myself. It's not helping the situation.

"Hey." He drops a careless kiss against the top of my head. "What are you two talking about?"

My face flames as the edges of Brooke's lips quirk with mischief.

I swear, if she takes matters into her own hands and lets the cat out of the bag, I'll kill her. I'm not even kidding. Brooke McAdams will end up being nothing more than a senseless statistic, and I'll walk away with zero regrets.

I shoot her a narrowed look that promises retribution.

"I'm trying to convince Sasha that she should go out with my cousin." She beams at him with an expression full of faux innocence. "Don't you think they'd be perfect for each other?"

He stares at her for a long moment. "Are you talking about Ryder?"

"Yup. That's the one."

His easy-going manner falls away as he frowns. "Actually, I think that's a shit idea."

"Oh?" She perks up like a bloodhound who's picked up a scent. "And why would that be?"

"Because he's a hockey player." He gives her a sharp look. "You know how those guys are."

Her expression turns icy. "Actually, I do. Kind of like the football players?"

Easton has the good grace to wince. "Yeah, I guess so," he mumbles, aware of the unfortunate circumstances surrounding her breakup.

"Anyway," she says before the moment can turn awkward, "Sash needs to get back into the dating game. It's been a while since her last," she pauses, and I'm almost afraid 'hookup' will shoot out of her mouth, "boyfriend. Maybe you can help convince her that she needs to sweep out the cobwebs every once in a while."

Oh my god. Please tell me she did not just say that.

If only the sidewalk would open up and swallow me whole. Let's hope a mental image hasn't come to his mind of what that would actually look like.

Easton's brows pinch together as he eyes me with a frown. "If you're looking for a guy, there are some nice ones in my English class. I could check with a couple of them and see if they're interested." Before I can formulate a response, he continues, "But stay away from the hockey players." There's a pause. "And the football players. You know what? Just stay away from the athletes in general. Then we won't have any problems."

Is he really trying to fix me up with other guys?

Even though I steel myself against the onslaught, a tidal wave of heartache crashes over me. If I'd been secretly holding out hope that Easton might feel something romantic toward me, it's clear from this five-minute convo that's not the case.

When I remain silent, he reiterates for a second time, "Just do me a favor and steer clear of Ryder." He glances in Brooke's direction. "You don't need to worry about Sasha's dating life. She'll get out there when she's good and ready."

Before Brooke can react, he says, "All right, I gotta take off." His gaze cuts back to mine. "You want to grab lunch later?"

Under normal circumstances, I'm always happy to spend time with Easton. After this enlightening discussion, however, I'm going to take a pass.

"No, sorry." I make up an excuse on the fly. "I need to meet with one of my professors about an assignment."

He shrugs as if it doesn't matter to him one way or the other.

It's yet another nail in the coffin.

"All right. I'll text you later." With a quick wave, he disappears through the crowd of students moving across campus.

Always one to strike when the iron is hot, Brooke clears her throat. "So, about Ry—"

"I'll do it," I snap before I can change my mind.

Her eyes widen as if not expecting my easy capitulation. "Really? You'll go out with him?"

I press my lips together until they feel bloodless and nod. "Yeah."

It's most likely a decision I'll end up regretting in the not-so-distant future, but that doesn't negate the fact that Brooke is right. I need to move on and stop holding out hope that Easton will ever see me as anything other than a friend.

2

EASTON

"Dude, I'm starving. Hurry the fuck up," Crosby bellows across the first floor of the house. "It's Tuesday and I'm in desperate need of tacos."

I shake my head before scooping up my keys and heading toward the front door.

"Woah, woah, woah. Why wasn't I invited? Everyone knows I like tacos." Asher tosses the Xbox controller onto the coffee table before rising to his feet. Disgruntled noises escape from the two blondes snuggled up against him.

"I didn't realize you needed a formal invitation." I hesitate in the entryway.

"You know what? Sometimes it might be nice to feel a little wanted. We've been in this relationship for three years and it doesn't feel like you appreciate me the same way you did in the beginning. In fact, I'd go so far as to say that you've been taking me for granted lately."

One side of my mouth quirks.

Fucking Asher.

I dip my head in acknowledgment. "Noted. I'll try to do better in the future."

His expression softens as he adds, "I appreciate that. In all honesty, I think we've both become complacent. Let's make a pact from here on out to make a little more time for each other."

I bite back the laughter that gurgles up in my throat. There is no way in hell I'm going to encourage this guy.

"Now that we've cleared that up, can we get moving? I'm pretty sure those tacos aren't going to eat themselves."

The girls rise expectantly to their feet.

"Can we come, too?" the bustier one asks.

When my roommate glances at me with a raised brow, I roll my eyes. "I don't care."

They beam in unison, looking like carbon copies of each other with their blonde hair, big boobs, toothy smiles, and long, sun-kissed legs. I'd be hard pressed to tell them apart. My teammate throws an arm over each of their shoulders as we head to my truck before piling in. Since there's about a dozen of us, the rest of the guys cram into Carson's decked-out Tahoe. The girls chatter incessantly about the mixer their sorority is throwing next weekend. After about five minutes, Crosby glances at me from the passenger seat before folding his fingers in the shape of a gun, placing two digits against his temple, and pulling the trigger.

Sadly, I have to agree.

It's a relief when we finally pull into the paved parking lot. I regret giving Asher the go ahead to let the girls tag along. I'm not going to be able to handle much more sorority talk, tacos or no tacos.

Asher is always surrounded by girls. The guy has more pussy than he knows what to do with. Most of the guys on the team are in the same position.

Hell, most of the time, I'm drowning in it myself.

As we head inside the brightly colored entrance, the group stops at the hostess station where a girl loiters behind a podium. Her head is bent as she stares at the phone in her palm like it's the most interesting thing she's ever seen.

When a handful of seconds crawl by without so much as an acknowledgment, Crosby shoots me an annoyed look. The guy wants his tacos, and he wants them now. I've seen him get hangry. It's not a pretty sight. He's like a baby who needs to be fed at regular intervals.

I clear my throat, but there's nothing. Not even a flicker of her eyes.

Growing impatient, Crosby shifts his weight from one foot to the other. The guy is on the verge of losing it.

Before that can happen, Asher says, "Excuse me? We'd like a table."

I expect the hostess to snap to attention with embarrassment and a profuse apology.

That doesn't happen. When she finally glances up, one brow is raised as if we're bothering her. Like she has no idea why a group of people might turn up at this restaurant around dinner time.

She takes a moment to glare at each of us in turn before her gaze narrows on Asher.

"Can I help you?" Boredom threads its way through her husky voice.

Asher blinks as if surprised by her prickly demeanor.

I'll be the first to admit this isn't the kind of reaction any of us are used to receiving. Most people go crazy when they come in contact with any of the Western Wildcats football players. We're like minor celebrities around here. I'm not saying I get off on it, I'm just stating facts.

But this girl doesn't seem to know who the hell we are. Or, if she does, she gives zero shits.

Undeterred by her lack of hospitality, Asher flashes his most charming smile. It's one that has sent hundreds of girls falling onto their backs before spreading their legs wide. If he has a superpower, that would be it. And he enjoys flexing it around campus with regularity. Especially if there's a hot girl in the vicinity.

My gaze bounces back to the female in question—the one who holds our dining options in her slender hands—to assess its impact.

Nada.

Hmmm. Well, that's certainly interesting.

It seems as if this girl is also in possession of a superpower. And that would be total immunity to Asher's charms.

Not only is she not impressed, but by the way the corners of her lips have wilted, she's pissed off that he even gave it the old college try.

I'm about to intervene when Crosby elbows me in my side none too gently. When I flick my gaze to him, he nods toward the packed dining area.

"Hey, isn't that Sasha?"

Doubtful. I texted her thirty minutes ago to see if she was interested in grabbing dinner and she responded that she was busy. So, no...I don't think—

My brows snap together when my gaze lands on her.

What the hell?

Did she seriously blow me off tonight?

I'm so focused on my best friend that it takes another moment to realize she's not alone at the table.

Before I can fully wrap my mind around that fact, Crosby cuts into my thoughts. "What's she doing with Ryder McAdams?"

Because yeah, that's exactly who she's with.

Damn it. And I know who's to blame for this.

The last thing Sasha needs is to get tangled up with a player. I don't realize that I'm on the move until I pull up to her booth and drop down on the seat next to her. My hip bumps into hers, nudging her over.

Eyes widening, she gasps, "Easton, what are you doing here?"

What am I doing here?

What am I doing here?

That's hilarious. I was just about to ask the same question. Sitting this close to her, it's impossible not to notice the cerulean color of her eyes. They're almost the exact shade of the Pacific Ocean. It's not like I didn't realize this before, but tonight they look bigger.

Brighter.

Maybe it's the dark shadow on her eyelids that makes them pop.

Wait a minute...

Since when does she wear makeup?

Or style her hair?

It's not that she doesn't always look nice, but Sasha plays soccer and spends a lot of time with her thick hair pulled back into a ponytail. She's never been one of those girls who constantly has a full face of makeup or her hair perfectly styled. I'll admit that I enjoy fucking those chicks, but they aren't the kind I want to eventually settle down with.

"Easton?"

It takes a moment to blink out of the strange thoughts that are tangling around me like jungle vines. "I could ask you the same thing."

Instead of giving me an answer, she rakes her teeth across the plumpness of her lower lip.

My gaze drops to the movement and a punch of need hits me full force, nearly knocking the breath from my lungs.

What the actual fuck?

It takes a moment to stomp out the arousal—

No—not arousal. It's protectiveness surging through me. Sasha has always been my best friend. It's for that very reason that I don't want to see her get wrapped up with Ryder. All he'll do is break her heart, and I'll be damned if I sit idly by and allow that to happen.

All of the noise and commotion surrounding us fades to the background as our gazes stay locked. I have no idea what to make of the peculiar energy crackling in the air between us. I've never experienced anything like it.

It's only when she blinks and glances across the table at the hockey player watching us with growing interest that I plummet back to Earth with a painful thud. The slow smirk curling around the corners of his lips instantly raises my hackles.

Sasha shifts before carefully inching away. Every centimeter of distance between us feels like a mile.

I don't like it.

It takes all of my willpower to stop myself from reaching out and dragging her closer.

Her hand flutters nervously as she gestures to the guy parked across from us. "Ryder asked if I wanted to go out for dinner."

When I continue to give him a well-honed death stare, the asshole actually has the audacity to grin as if this is some kind of game.

"Nice of you to crash our date, Clark. Why don't you take a load off and join us?"

Ignoring the sarcasm, I ground out between clenched teeth, "This isn't a date."

His gaze flickers to Sasha. "Sure, it is. Right, sweetheart?"

I throw my arm around her shoulders and haul her close just so he doesn't get any more delusional ideas. Although, by the looks of him, he's already got them.

That's all right. I have no problem beating them out of him. In fact, it would be my pleasure. But before I can crack my knuckles and rise to my feet, the guys I arrived with gather around the table.

There's a chorus of greetings before Carson waves me over. "Come on, man. They've got a table ready for us." With a scowl, he glances at Asher. "No thanks to this dumbass. If I had to guess by that chick's intense dislike for our man here," he slaps him on the back, "it must have been a fuck and flee situation. She would have refused us service if she could have gotten away with it."

Unsurprised, I shake my head before giving Sasha a little side-eye. There is no way in hell I'm abandoning ship and leaving her alone with this fuckwad.

"No need, there's more than enough room here." Sort of. "Why don't we join Sash and Ryder?"

Carson glances from me to the hockey player lounging on the seat across from us as if he doesn't have a care in the world. The blond football player's brows pull together as if he's assessing the situation before his attention once again settles on Sasha. "Are you sure you don't mind?"

"Umm—"

I squeeze her against me, cutting off her response. "Are you kidding? She doesn't mind at all."

Carson ponders this for a moment before shrugging. "Sure, all right then."

The booths are long enough that it's not a problem to squeeze three guys semi-comfortably in on one side. Asher and one of the sorority girls pile in beside Ryder, while Carson slides in next to me. Crosby pulls up two more chairs for himself and the other blonde. The rest of the guys grab a nearby table to camp out at.

Once we're all situated, the waitress arrives to take our order. It's unfortunately the same chick from the hostess station.

This doesn't bode well for us.

Or our tacos.

She takes her time going around the table, writing down everyone's order. When she gets to Asher, she gives us all a slight smile before swinging away.

"Hey," he calls out, deep voice rising above the noise in the dining room. "What about me?"

She spins around to face him before cocking a brow. "What about you?"

"I'd like to place an order." His voice hardens. "Is that going to be a problem?"

A thick blanket of tension settles over us as she shrugs and folds her arms across her chest. "I don't know. Is it?"

Instead of responding, his lips settle into a tight line as his eyes narrow. It's not an expression I've seen often from him. The guy is normally easy going and chill. He doesn't get bent out of shape over much. And why should he? Life has been pretty easy. From what I understand, he comes from money. Even though he's not the sharpest tool in the shed, he manages to skate through his classes each semester. And the girls flock to him like he's the pied piper of pussy. The guy must be a real rock star in the sack because his bed is never empty.

How do I know this?

I share a wall with him. One that has turned out to be paper thin. Let's just say I either make good use of my noise-canceling earphones or I'm forced to listen to the porn star soundtrack going on in the room next to me.

"I really hope not." There's a pause before he adds, "I'd hate to get your manager involved."

She bares her teeth like a rabid dog before snapping, "Fine. What do you want? And make it quick. I've got other customers to take care of."

Even though Asher knows exactly what he wants, he takes his sweet damn time perusing the menu. We've been here enough over the last three years to have memorized the plastic sheet. After a handful of moments, he strokes his shadowed jaw before glancing at her. "I can't remember if you mentioned any specials."

A muscle tics in her jaw. Any second, she's going to fly at him. "It's Tuesday, dickhead. That means all the tacos you can eat."

Everyone at the table stills, including Asher.

It's only when someone clears their throat from behind the waitress that everyone comes alive again. "Lola, can I talk to you for a moment?"

The words might be arranged in the format of a question, but by the flush on the older man's cheeks, it's more of a directive.

She stiffens as a dull flush crawls up her neck. "Yeah, give me a minute to put this order in." Her gaze stays laser focused on the blond football player who sparked her anger. "I assume you want the tacos."

"Yup."

When she swings away without another word, the older dude snaps, "Lola, don't you have something to say to this customer?" When she gives him a blank stare, he prompts, "Perhaps an apology for your unfortunate choice of language?"

She presses her lips together until they turn bloodless. Her nostrils flare as she sucks in a deep breath. "I'm sorry you're such a dickhead." That being said, she stalks away.

The older man wrings his hands as he glares at his disgruntled employee. "I'm, ah, sorry about that. She's..." His voice trails off as if he's at a loss for words.

"Got some serious issues going on?" Asher supplies in the silence.

The older man clears his throat, neither agreeing nor disagreeing with the statement. "Anyway...I'd like to apologize on behalf of our waitress for her unhospitable manner. That's not the Taco Loco way of treating customers. For your inconvenience, your meal will be on the house."

"Cool! Free tacos for everyone! Make sure to thank Lila for us!" Asher says, bouncing quickly back to his affable self.

I glance at Sasha as the table once again breaks out into conversation. She looks none too happy. Her lips are nothing more than a tight slash across her face. If I'd been looking to stomp out the flames of any budding romance that might ignite between these two, I've accomplished it with flying colors.

Even though I'm tempted to pat myself on the back for a job well done, I refrain.

For the time being, anyway.

3

SASHA

Brows pinched together, I glance around the crowded table in confusion.

How the hell did this happen?

One minute, I'm on a date, and the next, six more people are crammed in and around the booth. Instead of having a quiet conversation so I can get to know Ryder McAdams on a deeper level, football players are raising their voices in order to be heard at the neighboring table.

Easton's muscular arm is still draped over my shoulder, anchoring me to him. The woodsy scent of his aftershave continues to wrap slyly around me, teasing my—

No.

I refuse to go there. Tonight was supposed to be the first step in moving on from that unrequited situation. Instead, here I am, being inundated by his masculine presence. I pinch his thigh to get his attention. It doesn't escape me that he's been avoiding all eye contact for the last ten minutes.

When the first attempt goes unheeded, my fingers sink into his flesh and squeeze. When he glances at me, I whisper, "We need to talk."

"Sure. No problem. How about after dinner? The waitress should be bringing out our tacos any moment, and I'm starving." His gaze flickers to Asher. "And you know these guys won't bother to save any for us."

At the moment, I don't give a damn about the tacos. And since I'm of the mind that they belong in their own food group, that's saying a lot.

"Right now."

We engage in a staring contest for about fifteen seconds before he shrugs. It would be impossible not to notice how broad and perfectly sculpted his shoulders are. If I didn't know better, I'd say they were chiseled from marble. I shove those errant thoughts away before they can take root in my brain and mess any more with my hormones.

Carson slips from the booth before Easton slides over and rises to his feet. Before I can follow suit, his fingers lock around my wrist, pulling me up in one swift motion.

Embarrassed that my friends have ruined our date, I shift toward Ryder. This evening has turned out to be a total disaster, and it's doubtful anything will salvage it at this point. "I'll be right back."

"No worries," he says easily.

"I'm really—"

The apology perched on the tip of my tongue gets cut short as I'm dragged away from the table.

I stumble in my haste to keep up with him. "That was rude."

He snorts under his breath as we step into a short hallway where the bathrooms are located. The way his fingers singe the flesh of my wrist is enough to leave me lightheaded. Needing to break the physical connection pulsing between us, I twist out of his tight grip. It might have taken a while, but I've come to the realization that the only way to get over my feelings for Easton is to stomp them out every time they bubble to the surface.

Like right now.

It takes two attempts before he finally releases his hold.

I rub my wrist with delicate circles before backing away and flinging my hand toward the crowded dining room. "What was that all about?"

He shifts his stance as a frown settles across his features. "What do you mean? Joining you for dinner?"

Is he really that oblivious?

I roll my eyes and cross my arms over my chest. "Of course that's what I mean! Didn't you realize that we were on a date? Exactly how am I supposed to get to know Ryder if you and your friends are hijacking the conversation?"

"Last time I checked, they were your friends, too."

I squeeze my eyes closed and suck in a deep breath, hoping it will calm me from the inside out.

"That's not what I meant," I mutter as frustration pounds through me. "You crashed my date."

His eyes narrow as the edges of his lips sink. "Correction—what I did was save you from that loser. You looked bored off your ass, and I took it as a cry for help."

I shake my head. "A cry for help? Give me a break. I was having a good time. Ryder's a nice guy and he's actually really funny. He asked if I'd like to watch one of his games."

One brow rises. "Is that so?"

I blink at the abrupt change in his behavior.

Before I can figure out what it means, Easton stalks closer. My eyes widen as I scramble backward until my shoulders hit the wall and there's nowhere else to go. He's so close that I have to tip my chin to hold his steely gaze. My hands shoot out, both palms slamming into his chest to keep him from advancing any further.

The dark look in his eyes has my heart jackhammering painfully beneath my breast.

"He's not the right guy for you," he growls.

The way his voice dips, sounding as if it's been scraped from the bottom of the ocean, sends a fresh burst of nerves scampering down my spine.

"Why would you say that?" I can barely manage to force out the question.

"Because you don't need a guy who will toy with your heart. You need a man who can appreciate all the amazing qualities you have to offer. Like how smart, kind, and athletic you are. Or that you have a great sense of humor. Especially after a few drinks."

My lips quirk at the corners.

He picks up a thick lock of hair from my shoulder before rubbing it between his fingers. "And that you're absolutely gorgeous. I've always loved the way the sun glints off your hair when you wear it down. It's as dark and silky as a raven's wing."

A look of utter concentration enters his eyes as he continues to play with the strands. It's one that turns my mouth cottony. The moment stretches and lengthens until it feels like it could snap in half.

"Easton." The rasp of my voice is like a gunshot in the strained silence that surrounds us.

He blinks away the thick haze clouding his eyes. "Yeah?"

"What's going on here?"

Confusion flickers across his expression. "I don't know."

With his gaze pinned to mine, his face looms closer. Air gets wedged in my throat, making it impossible to breathe. Just as my eyelids feather shut, someone clears their throat from behind us. My eyes spring open, only to find Ryder standing a few feet away.

I shake my head and blurt, "It's not what it looks like."

He raises a brow as a smirk simmers across his lips. "Really? Because it kind of looked like Clark was about to kiss you."

Then it's exactly what it looks like.

But there's no way I can admit that.

"No, he was, ah..."

When my voice dies a slow, tortuous death, Ryder snorts out his derision. "I'm not looking to get in the middle of something. Brooke said you weren't involved. Clearly, she doesn't know what the hell she's talking about."

This just keeps getting worse.

"We're just friends!" I whisper, unable to meet Easton's gaze. What happened in the hallway was a mistake.

A weird moment that got out of hand.

Unconvinced by my stuttering and stammering, the blond hockey player hikes a thumb over his shoulder. "I'm gonna take off."

His words have me leaping into action. "No, wait!"

As I attempt to rush past Easton, his fingers wrap around my upper arm, halting me in my tracks.

"We need to talk." The low cadence of his voice does funny things to my insides.

That sounds like a terrible idea.

"Not right now." Talking will only complicate matters, and that's exactly what we don't need. The best thing we can do for our friendship is walk away from each other and pretend this little incident never happened.

Uncertainty flickers across his face and, for a heartbeat, it seems like he might argue. Instead, he jerks his head into a nod and releases my arm. I feel the loss of his touch the moment it falls away. A mixture of relief and regret spiral through me as I shoot out of the hallway like the hounds of hell are nipping at my heels.

4

———————

EASTON

A couple hours later, I lift a bottle of beer to my lips and take a long swig. The icy brew does nothing to dull the confusion rampaging through me. And the dark-haired girl with the big blue eyes who parked herself on my lap isn't helping matters either. The way her nimble fingers drift lazily over my chest should have something stirring south of the border.

It doesn't.

In fact, the longer I stare, the more she reminds me of a certain someone else who shall remain nameless.

Even though I'm not turned on in the least, it's tempting to take this girl upstairs and fuck her brains out.

Slender hands stroke over my chest and up my shoulders before long nails scrape the back of my neck. Her tongue peeks out to moisten her lips as her eyelids lower to half-mast. "Wanna take this little party upstairs for a while?"

When I remain silent, she presses closer and nibbles at my throat.

A month or so ago, you wouldn't have had to ask twice. I would have happily scooped this Sasha look-alike up and carried her to my bedroom.

Now, however, the thought of actually doing that leaves a pit the

21

size of Texas sitting at the bottom of my gut. I have zero interest in screwing a chick who resembles my best friend. In fact, I have a sneaking suspicion that it would only make matters worse.

What the hell is going on with me?

Where did all these strange thoughts and feelings come from?

I've never felt anything other than friendship for her. We grew up together. When I got into mischief, Sasha was always my sidekick. We had standing plans to sneak out of our houses every Saturday night to attend high school parties. She's had a slew of boyfriends, and I've had...

Girls who knew I wasn't interested in a commitment and were totally cool with that.

Over the years, I've gone to great lengths to never think about her in that light. She's always been a friend who just so happened to be a chick.

After all these years, why is this happening now when we're seniors in college and will graduate this spring? We've got a ton going on. She's in the process of applying for grad school and looking for employment opportunities. My father owns his own residential construction company, and the plan has always been for me to take over one day. A degree in business management will help with that. I'll probably end up going back to school in the not-so-distant future for my MBA, but I want to get a little work experience under my belt first. Sasha spent the last two summers interning for Dad. He's been trying to persuade her to join the company. Our families and lives will always be entwined. The worst thing I could do is fuck up our relationship by doing something we'll both regret.

"Easton?"

It takes a moment to blink back to the present and the perturbed girl sitting on my lap.

Well, fuck. I almost forgot about her.

That's a first.

The way her brows pinch together along with the frown that now mars her expression tells me it's a first for her as well.

Naomi is a gorgeous girl. Exactly the type I normally go for.

Stacked on top with a big ass and a nipped-in waist. She's like a wet dream come to life.

Except...I'm kind of wishing her body was tighter. More muscular. Athletic.

More like—

Nope. Don't even go there.

I drag a hand over my face to banish the wayward thoughts, but it doesn't do a damn bit of good. There's only one girl I want to spend time with. And it's not the one attempting to claim my distracted attention.

"Easton, are you all right?"

I shake my head before setting down the bottle and loosening her grip. I'm more than aware this will take some delicate maneuvering on my part. "No. I think it might be the tacos I wolfed down earlier. They're not sitting well."

A look of horror flashes across her pretty features. "Oh my god, are you going to throw up?"

Now that she mentioned it...

I nod solemnly. "It's a definite possibility."

The color in her cheeks drains. "Yeah...I can't be around someone who's sick. Even the thought of it makes me gag." She scampers off my lap before carefully backing away like I've just been diagnosed with syphilis.

"Okay, well..." She stabs a finger toward the dining room where a bunch of people have congregated. "I'm just gonna see what Megan is up to."

A smile trembles around the corners of my lips. That was easier than anticipated. "No worries."

"Text me when you're feeling better," she calls over her shoulder before disappearing into the crowd.

"Sure." By the time the response leaves my lips, Naomi is long gone. My guess is that she's moving on to greener pastures. I can't blame her for not sticking around to make sure I'm all right. It's not like we're in a relationship. Or even know each other that well. When it comes right down to it, we're fuck buddies.

That notion has never bothered me before, but now…

I don't know.

For some reason, it does. I could go upstairs and puke my guts out and this girl wouldn't give a goddamn. She'd walk over my heaving body to get to the next football player who looked sideways at her.

I shake my head to clear it of the bizarre thoughts that have taken up residence inside my brain.

Seriously. What the hell is going on with me tonight?

"Hey, are you okay?" Brayden parks himself on the couch across from the velour chair I'm sprawled out on. Music pulses from the speakers in the dining room. "I just ran into Naomi. She said something about you having food poisoning and hurling all over the place."

I roll my eyes before glancing around cautiously and admitting, "I told her that so she'd take off."

He raises a brow before guzzling down a quarter of his water. "Well, mission accomplished. It's doubtful she'll ever look twice in your direction again."

"That's fine by me." As the flippant words escape from my mouth, I realize that I mean them. Naomi is no different than any of the other groupies who hang around the house. They're a dime a dozen.

My teammate studies me for a long moment. With any other guy, it might be uncomfortable, but I've known Brayden since football camp the summer after high school graduation. Three years later, he's turned out to be a good friend. One I can count on. One I can be honest with.

Maybe.

"So, what you're telling me is that we don't have a taco emergency on our hands?"

I shake my head. "Nope. You don't have to worry about them making an encore appearance anytime soon."

"Good to know. If it's not bad Mexican, then what's the problem?" There's a pause as he studies me. "You seem kind of off."

I glance away. He's not telling me anything I don't already know. I *am* off. Now that I'm thinking about it, I realize it's been that way for a while. "Yeah, I'm aware."

Even though I mumble the words under my breath, he still manages to hear them.

"There's obviously something on your mind." When I remain silent, he makes an impatient gesture with his hand. "Come on, spit it out so we can both move on with our lives."

I shoot him a glare, wishing it were that simple. Nothing feels easy about this situation I now find myself in.

Another minute ticks by before I force myself to admit, "There's a girl—a friend—who I might be interested in."

His brows rise as he straightens on the chair. "Holy shit. You like Sasha?"

"I never said that," I fire back, cheeks heating with embarrassment.

He points a finger in my direction. "You certainly didn't deny it."

Well, he's got me there.

"Fine," I grumble. "It's Sash."

A grin stretches across his face. "Now, was that really so difficult to admit?"

"Kind of."

He snorts. "So you like Sasha. Why is this a problem?"

"I'm not sure it is."

"All right, let's break this down. Is she aware that you have special feelings for her?"

I scrunch my nose. Is this guy serious? "Special feelings?"

"Yeah. Like, you don't just want to hold her hand, you want her to give you a handy."

This conversation is starting to feel like a mistake.

When I remain silent, Brayden bursts out laughing. "I'm just kidding. God...the look on your face is priceless."

Definite mistake.

Before I can backtrack from the discussion, Brayden says, "All joking aside, I get it. Your feelings for Sasha have changed and you're wondering if you should do something about it. You're friends—good friends—and you don't want to ruin that."

My shoulders collapse under the weight of his words. In a nutshell...

"That's exactly it."

His lips lift into a knowing smile. "See how easy that was?"

Easy my ass.

"What are you looking for? A little bit of advice?"

"Yeah, I guess I am." It can't hurt, right?

Don't answer that.

"Here are my thoughts on the matter." There's a pause. "If you think this is a passing thing, then keep it to yourself. There's no reason to ruin a perfectly good friendship over a bit of attraction that will probably end up fizzling out."

My mouth turns bone dry. What is he saying? That I should keep these newly realized feelings to myself and hope they disappear?

Before I can ask for clarification, he continues, "But, if you think Sasha could be the girl who changes everything for you," his gaze flickers over the sea of people filling the first floor of our house and I imagine that he's searching for his newly minted girlfriend, "then you gotta take a chance." His attention zeros in on me again. "Because it's worth it."

The last thing I want to do is ruin our decades long friendship, but I also don't want to miss out on something that could be amazing because I was too chickenshit to take a chance.

I'll be the first to admit that I don't know a damn thing about love.

Sasha is the only girl I've ever had strong feelings for. If she's out celebrating, I want to be by her side, cheering her on. If she's sad or upset, I want to be the one who makes her feel better. If she's struggling with an issue, I want to be the one who swoops in and solves it. Not that she needs me to step in and take over, but still...I want to be the one she turns to no matter what's going on in her life.

When it comes down to it, I just want to be with her.

No matter what's going on.

I straighten on the chair as that thought crashes unexpectedly through my head.

Well, shit.

Sasha has been standing in front of me this entire time and I never realized it. Never even considered the possibility that we could be more than friends.

Until now.

"What are you going to do?" Brayden asks, cutting into the whirl of my thoughts.

I shake my head. In the past, the path I've always needed to take has been clear. There have never been any questions as to how I'm going to proceed. But this...

"I'm not sure." The dilemma continues to roll around inside my head. What I do know is that Sasha and I fit together perfectly. She's my other half.

But what if she doesn't feel the same way?

What if she thinks we're better off as friends?

What then?

SASHA

"Want me to pause the movie while you get that?"

I glance at Ryder, who lounges on the couch beside me before popping to my feet as another insistent knock comes from the other side of the apartment door.

"If you don't mind, that would be great."

With one click of the remote, the television screen freezes as I quickly pad into the small entryway. I have no idea who could be pounding on the door at this time of night.

I peer through the peephole before stumbling away. With a quick step in retreat, I glance over my shoulder at the guy in the living room. It took fifteen solid minutes to convince him that Easton and I are nothing more than friends and that there's never been anything remotely romantic between us. Him showing up uninvited on my doorstep at ten at night won't reinforce that notion.

I nibble my lower lip and try to decide what to do.

There's always the possibility that if I ignore him, he'll go away. Relief slides through me as the knocking abruptly comes to a halt. Tomorrow will be soon enough to deal with Easton. Right now, I want to spend time with Ryder.

Before I can swing around and rejoin my date on the couch, a deep voice says, "Sash? Are you in there?"

"Is everything all right?" Ryder calls from the living room at the same time.

Damn.

Damn.

Damn.

There's no way I can remain silent.

"Yup, everything's fine," I call back, anxiety tinging my voice, making it sound high pitched and reedy. "Just give me a minute."

"Sash," Easton growls, voice turning insistent, "let me in right now."

I open the door just enough to slip into the hallway without allowing him to catch a glimpse inside before closing it behind me. My hand remains wrapped around the handle.

"Um, hey...what are you doing here?" A fresh wave of nerves skitters down my spine before invading my voice, giving it a fine tremble that's difficult to hide.

"We need to clear the air." His gaze stays pinned to me. The heavy weight of his stare makes it impossible to breathe.

"Yeah, sure." I pause as my head continues to spin. "How about we tackle that tomorrow when we're both clear headed?" And Ryder is nowhere in the vicinity.

He huffs out a breath before shifting his stance. "That's the thing. For the first time in my life, I feel like I'm actually thinking clearly." He nods toward my apartment. "Can we go inside and talk? I don't want to have this conversation in the hallway."

Frantically, I try to come up with an excuse as to why that can't happen. "You know what? I'm exhausted. I was just about to hit the sack." I feign a yawn. "Maybe we could meet up and grab a coffee tomorrow morning before classes?"

Easton frowns as he glances at his phone. "It's not even ten. You usually stay up until at least midnight."

"Yeah-yeah, I know. But it's been a long week. Practice really kicked my ass." My hand flutters between us like a hummingbird on crack. "You know how it is."

For a long moment he stares at me before his eyes narrow. "Is there any reason you don't want me to come inside?"

Oh crap.

I've never been able to lie to Easton. At least, not successfully.

"Um, no?" My brows rise as I force out the last syllable.

"Why does that sound more like a question?"

"Umm..." That's the moment my brain decides to take a hiatus.

He straightens to his full height, every muscle tensing. "Is Ryder here?"

Even though the words are arranged into a question, we both know the answer.

Anger flashes through his eyes like lightning. I gulp and quickly remind myself that I don't owe Easton any explanations for my behavior. We're friends. Nothing more. Nothing less. I'm free to do as I please, just as he is.

Have I ever said anything about all the girls he gets with?

Nope. Not a word.

That thought has me jerking my shoulders back, straightening to my full height and crossing my arms tightly against my chest. "As a matter of fact, he is." When Easton's expression darkens, I shift awkwardly beneath his relentless glower. "We're watching a movie."

"And?" He arches a brow as if waiting for more.

"And what?"

When I remain silent, he growls, "Has he tried anything?"

I blink.

Is this guy being serious?

The muscles that tic in his tightly clenched jaw tell me that he is. My mouth turns cottony, making it difficult to swallow. I can't help but shift restlessly beneath his penetrating stare.

When his intense scrutiny becomes too much to withstand, I blurt, "No."

Relief floods his expression, and his shoulders loosen. "Good. Now tell Ryder to go home."

"What? No!" Is he out of his mind? Easton can't waltz in here and tell me what to do.

He tips his head toward the apartment. "If you don't, I will."

"Why are you being so unreasonable? What the hell has gotten into you today?" If I didn't know better, I'd think he'd been invaded by body snatchers. My best friend has always been laid back and easy going. The guy standing before me, demanding that I put a swift end to my date, doesn't resemble him in the slightest. It's like they're not even the same person.

"Like I said before, I've finally come to my senses," he mutters as if that statement will somehow shed light on our current disagreement. "Now get rid of him."

We glare for a good fifteen seconds before I realize he isn't going to back down anytime soon.

"All right," I reluctantly mutter before adding, "but only because we need to hash out whatever is going on here."

"As long as McAdams gets the fuck out of your apartment, I don't care what you tell yourself the reason is."

The feral smile that curves his lips has arousal bursting to life at the bottom of my belly. If I'm being completely honest, the ignition is much lower. The way our gazes stay fastened sends my pulse skyrocketing. It flutters madly against the delicate flesh of my throat. His eyes darken until it feels like I'm in imminent danger of drowning in their expressive depths.

When his fingers lift, feathering along the curve of my jaw, an unexpected shiver works its way through me as he strokes the side of my face. A tidal wave of sensation crashes over me before threatening to drag me to the very bottom of the ocean.

For as long as I can remember, it's been Easton. All of my secret thoughts and dreams have revolved around him.

And that's a problem.

These caresses might be innocent and meaningless to him, but they mean everything to me. They grab hold of my insides and draw me closer, making it difficult to distance myself. To keep him firmly in the friend zone where he was always meant to be.

Before I can lose myself completely in his touch, my fingers tighten around the door handle and twist. When it springs open, I tumble backward with a squeak. The haze clouding his eyes clears before he jumps into action. He grabs my upper arms and yanks me forward until I'm trapped against the steely strength of his chest. It's oh-so-tempting to close my eyes and burrow against him. Nothing about this moment should feel right.

"Oh, for fuck's sake," a deep voice snaps, slicing into my thoughts and catapulting me back to the present with a painful thud. "I should have realized when I found you two in the hallway at Taco Loco that tonight would turn out to be a total bust."

A groan of embarrassment gurgles up from my throat.

When I attempt to break free, Easton traps me against him, making escape impossible.

"Say goodbye to Ryder," he whispers against the shell of my ear. The heat of his breath sends a torrent of shivers dancing down my spine. "And while you're at it, tell him to lose your number."

Instead of doing exactly that, I clear my throat and force myself to say, "I'm really sorry about tonight."

His expression softens, making him look less irritated. Certainly less annoyed than I would be if the situation were reversed.

"Don't worry about it. Brooke's been on my ass for a while to take you out. After the clusterfuck this night has been, she owes me big time."

That last comment makes me wince as he saunters past, leaving a heavy silence in his wake.

It's only when we're alone that Easton releases his hold before nudging me inside the apartment and closing the door behind us. A strange intensity fills his eyes. It's one that has my belly crashing to the bottom of my toes. I've known him forever, and not once has he ever frightened me. But at this particular moment, that's exactly how I feel. I have no idea how this interaction will play out, and that leaves me feeling off kilter and unsure how to smooth everything over.

"Easton," I whisper, unable to summon my voice.

When my tongue darts out to moisten my lips, his gaze drops to the movement and a groan rumbles up from deep in his chest as he stalks closer. The fine hair on my arms prickles with awareness when he grinds to a halt before reaching out and cradling my cheeks in his palms.

"I'm sorry."

I blink in confusion. "For what?"

"For not realizing what I felt sooner."

Everything inside me stills, and it takes effort to push out the question. "And what is it you feel?"

"That there's something between us that I've never had with any other girl. Anyone period. You mean everything to me." The energy swirling around us ratchets up to unprecedented levels. It's both terrifying and exhilarating all at the same time. "What I'm trying to say is that I like you, Sash."

Sash.

It's always been his nickname for me. But it's never meant more than it does in this moment.

Not in a million years did I expect this confession. "You do?"

His thumb strokes leisurely over my lower lip. The delicate motion scatters all of my thoughts, making it impossible to think straight.

My heart thumps a painful staccato against my ribcage. I won't pretend that I haven't fantasized about this moment unfolding between us dozens of times. For years, it's felt like I've been standing on the sidelines, quietly watching him. Yearning for something that was never meant to be.

In my dreams, I would leap into his arms and everything would fall neatly into place. What I didn't imagine was that fear and anxiety would bubble up inside me, dampening any of my joy.

"If I'm being a hundred percent honest, I think these feelings have been simmering beneath the surface for a while. I was too..." His voice trails off before he straightens his shoulders, his expression turning to one of resolve. "I was too chickenshit to acknowledge them."

His nervousness only heightens my own, making me acknowledge there's more at stake than I originally realized.

When I remain silent, he whispers, "Tell me you feel the same way."

That's exactly what I want to do. But…how can I take a chance and possibly lose our friendship?

Regret swallows me whole as my teeth scrape across my lower lip.

"Sasha?" A desperate edge creeps into his voice.

It takes everything I have inside to shake my head.

Shock floods his features and his eyes widen. "No?"

I glance away, forcing myself to admit the truth. "We've always been such great friends. Best friends," I emphasize, gaze locking on his. "I don't want to lose that. I don't want to lose *you*."

"But—"

"We've known each other forever," I say, voice rising. "And in all that time, you've never gotten serious with anyone. Not even in high school."

"Maybe that's true," he concedes, shoulders collapsing. "But that doesn't mean I don't want to give this a shot."

It's almost painful to realize how much I want to believe him. What worries me is that the odds of a relationship working out aren't in our favor. Would we be able to remain friends afterward? Could life go back to what it's always been? He means too much to me, and the thought of him not being my best friend, the guy I can share everything with, scares the crap out of me.

"I think it would be for the best if we keep our relationship platonic." Emotion rushes through me, fighting to break free. It's all I can do to keep the tears that burn the back of my eyelids at bay.

"I can't do that," he growls, dragging my face closer until the warmth of his breath drifts over my parted lips.

"Easton…"

My voice dies a quick death when his mouth crashes onto mine. Every protest clamoring inside me is instantly silenced. When his tongue peeks out to tease the seam of my lips, I keep them pressed together, knowing that if the kiss turns deeper, I'll be lost. Swept away on a turbulent sea of longing. A rumble of displeasure erupts from him when I continue to resist his advances.

He pulls away just enough to growl, "Open for me."

And then he's back again, storming my defenses and demanding entrance. He nips at my lower lip with sharp teeth, and I gasp at the unexpected sizzle of pleasure-infused pain. That second of stunned surprise is all it takes for him to force his way inside until his tongue can tangle with my own.

With his hands cupping the sides of my face, he angles my head in order to gain better access. A whimper escapes from me as he changes the angle and slows things down. Now that the floodgates are open, it's impossible to hold back or pretend that I don't want this. That I haven't wanted it for years. My arms twine around his neck, pulling him closer until my breasts are crushed against the hard lines of his chest.

The way his mouth roves hungrily over mine, sampling it like he'll never get enough weakens my knees. Any moment, I'm going to melt into a pile of heated wax at his feet. I've imagined what it would be like to kiss Easton hundreds of times—maybe more—but all of those daydreams have been reduced to a paper tiger in comparison to the reality.

"You taste so damn sweet," he mutters.

His hands drift from my cheeks to my shoulders before slowly sliding down the side of my ribcage to my waist where his fingers curl, biting into my flesh. Arousal explodes in my core as he drags me close enough to feel his cock digging into the softness of my belly. When his hands fall from my waist over the curve of my hip before settling on my backside, another burst of need explodes in me. He tightens his hold, squeezing the firm flesh as if he'll never release it.

Easton breaks away long enough to search my eyes with a heavy-lidded gaze that burns with intensity before lifting me into his arms. My head spins as he swings around and carries me through the tiny dining area before arriving in my room. With his foot, he kicks the door shut and deposits me on the bed.

My heart jackhammers as I bounce on the mattress before settling. My legs are stretched out in front of me, knees slightly bent as I prop myself up with my elbows. My attention stays focused on him as his fingers grip the hem of his Navy T-shirt and yank it up, revealing perfectly sculpted abdominals and pectorals.

Once he tosses the cottony material to the carpet, he stalks closer. My nerves ratchet up with every step. His wide palms find the bed as he crawls up my body until his mouth is able to align with mine. My elbows collapse under his weight until I'm stretched out flat as he hovers over me. We still as our breaths mingle. It's a drugging sensation.

Carefully, he presses his lips against the corner of my mouth before giving the same ardent attention to the other side. And then it's like the floodgates open as he rains sweet kisses over every inch of my face.

"You can't begin to understand how much I want you," he groans between caresses. "I told myself that I didn't, but it was a lie. One I've been trying to convince myself of for a while now."

It's everything I've always wanted to hear, but still...I can't help the fear that leaps to life deep inside me.

"I don't want to lose you," I whisper in the darkness of the room.

"There's no way you'll ever lose me." He rolls to the side before settling next to me. His fingers flirt with the bottom of my shirt where they hesitate. "Do you trust me?"

That's not a question I have to ponder. There has never been a time in my life when I didn't have absolute faith in Easton. Anywhere he led, I would blindly follow.

I nod.

"You realize I would never do anything to hurt you, right?"

The air trapped at the back of my throat rushes from my body in a burst. "I do."

That admittance has my muscles loosening and I sink into the softness. Easton gathers up the fabric of my shirt before carefully dragging it up my body and over my head, dropping it to the floor. His fingers return, slipping around the sides of my ribs before finding the latch in the middle of my back. I arch, giving him room to maneuver until the stretchy material snaps apart and he's able to remove it, leaving me as bare-chested as he is.

Nerves explode in me, making me aware of my unclothed state. No matter how close we've been, he's never seen my naked breasts.

It's almost impossible to remain still beneath the heavy burn of his gaze as it roves over me. I don't realize that I've lifted my arms in an attempt to cover myself until his fingers lock around my wrists, halting my movements.

"Don't. I want to look at you." His voice is deep and low. "You're so fucking beautiful."

My nipples tighten beneath his heavy-lidded gaze. It's all the invitation he needs to reach out. A gasp escapes from me when his heated palms cover me entirely, testing the soft weight before disappearing. A second after the cool air wafts over my flesh, his thumb and forefinger lock around the stiff peaks, gently pinching them in tandem until my back is bowing off the mattress.

Arousal spirals through every nerve ending, lighting me up from the inside out. It's like he knows exactly how to touch me to elicit an avalanche of pleasure. Most guys are more interested in themselves and their own gratification. That's not the case with Easton. His focus remains locked on me as he toys with my breasts, alternating between squeezing the plump flesh and tweaking the little buds until I'm writhing beneath him.

Just when I can't stand another second of this sweet torture, his large hands drift over my ribcage and belly before settling at the waistband of my jeans. His gaze, which had been following the path of his hands, lifts to mine in silent question.

It's one that has the potential to change the trajectory of our entire friendship.

6

EASTON

*A*ir gets wedged in my lungs as my attention remains locked on hers. I don't think I've ever wanted anything more in my life than I want Sasha. But she has to want it, too. This can't be something she feels forced into.

Unable to resist exploring more, my fingertips slip beneath the waistband of her jeans in order to graze the soft skin beneath the material. This isn't the first time I've laid hands on Sasha, but there has never been this level of intimacy between us. The feel of her, the breathy little sounds that escape from her are nothing short of addictive.

I want more.

No...I want everything.

Every sound. Every burst of pleasure.

I want it all.

"All you have to do is say the word and we'll stop." I force out the rest. "I'll leave, and we'll forget this ever happened." When she remains silent, the tension ratchets up inside me to unprecedented levels. In the past, when I've fooled around with a girl, I didn't care if she put the kibosh on what we were doing because I knew there would be another female waiting to take her place. What's happening here couldn't feel more different. This matters. *She* matters. "Is that what you want?"

My fingers still as I wait for her response.

When she shakes her head, the thick tension that had gathered in my shoulders evaporates as relief surges through me.

"Say the words," I growl. "I need to hear them."

"I don't want you to leave, but that doesn't mean I'm not scared."

"I know, baby. I promise everything will be all right." Even though I have no way of knowing if that statement is true, I've never been more certain of anything in my life. It's crazy the way your eyes can be opened and everything around you is suddenly different, never to be the same again.

This is one of those moments.

Wanting to reassure her, my fingers slip from her jeans. I move over her upper body, caging her in so that my mouth can settle on hers. The moment our lips collide, she opens, and my tongue delves inside. This time, there is no hesitancy. And that is such a fucking turn on.

I nip at her lower lip before drawing the plump flesh into my mouth. A whimper escapes from her when I finally release it with a soft pop. My teeth scrape against the curve of her jaw before meandering down the slender column of her throat to her collarbone. My lips hover over one taut peak before pulling it deep into my mouth. Need ricochets through me as her hands drift to my shoulders. Her fingers bite into my bare flesh as I release her nipple, moving to the other one and giving it the same attention. I could play with her like this all night and not grow tired of it. But there's so much more to explore. More I'm greedy to discover.

My movements sink lower as I pepper kisses against her ribs and over her belly before reaching her jeans. I glance up, holding her gaze as my fingers make quick work of the button and zipper before I'm sliding the thick material down her hips and thighs until there's nothing but a thin scrap of fabric to hide her from me.

Now that we've broken down most of the barriers, I can't stand for anything to come between us. My fingers slip beneath the delicate fabric at her hipbones before gradually revealing what lies beneath. My cock stiffens as her silky-soft mound comes into view. An inch more and her pussy is exposed. It only takes a few seconds to strip away her panties until she's totally bare.

Holy fuck.

With my palms pressed against her knees, I force them apart. Even though I've been with my fair share of girls over the years, this is the first time I've ever wanted to take my time and savor the moment, soaking up all the little details. It's the need to take this slow that makes me realize how different this experience is from all the others that have come before it.

Carefully, I raise one leg until I can slip between them. My hands slide from the inside of her knees to the supple skin of her inner thighs. Her gaze stays pinned to mine as my fingers stroke over her center, trailing from the bottom of her slit to the top of her mound and back again. I don't stop caressing her until she's shifting impatiently beneath my hands. Only then do I lower my mouth so that my breath can ghost over her delicate flesh. When she shudders, straining to get closer, I spread her lips so that my tongue can dance over her clit.

The tortured whimper that escapes is music to my ears. Her fingers tunnel through my hair in an attempt to lock me in place.

"You taste so damn good, baby." I don't think I've ever tasted anything so delectable in my life.

It doesn't take long before her muscles tighten and her hips lift. I circle her clit, applying more pressure until she cries out, shattering beneath my touch. Her inner muscles spasm as I lap at her shuddering softness. With a sigh, she melts bonelessly into the mattress. I press one last kiss against her before crawling up her body. My cock is so fucking hard. All I want to do is rip off the athletic shorts and boxers that separate us before sliding deep inside the warmth of her body.

Instead, I roll onto my side and take her with me so she's sprawled across my bare chest. My heart feels like it's going to pound right out of my ribcage. I'm so fucking turned on that it's painful. It wouldn't surprise me if the tip of my dick blew off. After spending weeks not feeling much of anything in that department, this is a revelation. One I don't ever want to let go of.

For a long moment, we lay wrapped in each other's arms. The silence that settles around us isn't uncomfortable, but it's different than what it's always been. Something new has been born this night.

Sasha lifts her head to study me. Even in the darkness, I see the questions that lurk in her eyes. "Should we talk about this?"

I shake my head. "Nope. We can do that in the morning."

"But—"

My fingers slide through her inky-colored strands before I draw her face to mine, silencing any further conversation between us. Only when her body relaxes do I draw away and pull her back to my chest.

Which is exactly how we fall asleep.

7

—————

SASHA

My eyelids flutter open as I gradually wake to my surroundings. When was the last time I felt this well rested? It's like I just had the best sleep of my life. As I stretch, my arm knocks into a hard slab of—

Muscle.

That's the moment I realize I'm not alone. All of the pleasant fuzziness clouding my brain evaporates. Carefully, I swivel my head until my gaze lands on a naked male chest. That's when everything from the night before rushes in and I'm bombarded with the reality of this situation.

Easton.

He stayed over and—

A rush of heat fills my cheeks.

Went down on me.

Even thinking about the way he touched my body ignites a firestorm of need inside me. My inner thighs clench in an unconscious attempt to stifle the sensation inundating my system, but it doesn't help.

My fingers rise until they can drift across my lips. In all the years

42

we've been friends, he's never kissed me like that. There have been pecks here and there, but nothing like last night.

As I shift against the sheets, I'm reminded of my naked state. Afterward, I thought about pulling on a tank top and underwear, but I was too comfortable to move a single muscle. Careful not to disturb him, I lift the sheet and peek beneath the cotton, only to catch an eyeful. Some time during the night, his boxers and shorts were shed.

My teeth sink into my lower lip, pinning it in place as my attention stays fixated on his length. Even in repose, he's big. I've had my fair share of guys, and he's one of the more...er, girthier ones I've seen. It's all too tempting to inspect him closer.

Our families have taken trips together and I've seen him countless times in boardshorts, but I've never caught a glimpse of him in the buff. Without a doubt, he's a sight to behold.

A gasp escapes from me when he moves and his cock stiffens, rising to a full-on salute.

Holy cow. Yeah, he's...*big.*

"Like what you see?"

The low timbre of his voice strums something deep inside me and arousal bursts to life in my core. If I were wearing panties, they'd be soaked. I slam the sheet back into place, although that does nothing to hide the boner tenting the material.

How embarrassing. I've just been caught ogling my best friend. That thought drives home the gravity of our situation. What happened last night was a mistake. As nice as it was—oh, who am I kidding? It was much better than nice. Hands down, it was one of the best orgasms of my life, and we didn't even have sex. But still...

How stupid would it be to jeopardize our friendship?

It was a heat-of-the-moment kind of thing. Maybe a spark of jealousy ignited inside him when he saw me with Ryder. I have no idea. What I do know is that it can't happen again. One time can be chalked up as an error in judgment. Anything more...

And we'll be careening down a path neither of us is prepared to deal with.

Before I can toss off the covers and scramble from the bed, Easton shackles my wrists and cages me in with the heavy weight of his body.

"Oh, no you don't." Heat ignites in his eyes as a slow smirk curves his lips. "How did I know you would try to run from me?" One muscular thigh gets thrown over my legs to keep me pinned in place. His thick erection presses insistently against my hip. "Now that I've had a taste of you, there's no way I'll give it up."

No matter how much I try to steel myself against the desire he sparks to life so easily, it's impossible. A whimper explodes from me as another wave of heat dampens my core.

I say the only thing I can to stop this from happening.

"Do you have any idea how much I love you? The friendship we have is special."

The heat filling his eyes vanishes as softness rushes in to fill the void. "I love you too, Sash. You know that. Maybe that love is morphing into something new, but that's all right."

"What if it doesn't? What if we're only meant to be friends? I don't want to lose you."

"That will never happen. Do you understand me?" His lips ghost over mine. "We'll take this slow, okay? One day at a time."

He breaks away long enough for our gazes to lock. A silent promise is transmitted between us before his lips return, wiping away the doubts that have mushroomed up inside me.

"We won't take this any further until you're ready."

Relief floods through me as I nod.

In order for a romantic relationship to have any chance of succeeding, that's exactly what needs to happen. And it gives me hope that we're both on the same page.

8

EASTON

"Dude, you need to settle," Rowan says, walking past on the way to his locker.

I roll my head from side to side as if that will alleviate the nerves eating away at my insides.

"What's up with him?"

From the corner of my eye, I catch Rowan nodding toward me.

Brayden, who's in the middle of getting dressed, sends a speculative glance in my direction.

"If I had to guess, I'd say it was a female."

The quarterback glances at me. "Is that right? Who's the lucky—or maybe I should say unlucky—girl?"

Like I'm going to answer that question.

If I know these assholes—and I do—they'll bust my balls if they realize who has me worked up into a series of complicated little knots, and then I'll never hear the end of it. Although, if any of my teammates should understand, it would be these two. Both of them have fallen hard and fast.

When Brayden grins like a Cheshire cat, the conversation we had the other night slams into me full force.

Well, hell.

"E has a hard-on for Sasha."

Rowan's brows rise at that bit of information. "No way."

I glare at Brayden for turning something important into nothing more than a joke. That's the last thing I need. Practice ran over by twenty minutes and I'm already late to pick her up for our date. I'm doing my best to prove that not only can we be the best of friends, but lovers as well. Sasha has always been my everything. I feel like a complete idiot for not seeing how perfect we were for each other sooner. I don't know what the hell I'd been thinking. Maybe I should thank Ryder for forcing me to confront the feelings that have been brewing for a while now.

On second thought...

"My guess is that Clark has it bad." He yanks up his boxers before glancing my way. "I assume you straightened out your situation the other night?"

Fucker.

Disappointment settles on Rowan's face as he shakes his head. "Looks like I owe Demi twenty bucks. She figured it wouldn't be much longer before you two realized that you were more than friends."

My mouth tumbles open. "Are you serious?"

He shrugs. "Yeah, she called it about a month ago. I told her she was crazy, but apparently that girl can see things I don't."

How the hell could Demi realize what was going on when I couldn't?

Rowan claps me on the shoulder, drawing my attention back to him. "Anyway man, congrats. Sasha's a cool chick."

"Yeah, she is," I mutter, still knocked off balance.

He cocks his head. "So, you two are headed out tonight?"

"Yeah." I glance at the digital clock on the wall above the door. "I'm late. I was supposed to pick her up ten minutes ago."

"Then I guess you'd better get your ass in gear."

He's right. Even though there hasn't been much to this conversation, it's settled something deep inside me.

It takes less than five minutes for me to dress, grab my athletic bag, and head out the door. I send Sasha a quick text to let her know that I'm on my way before sliding behind the wheel of my truck.

I've pulled out all the stops tonight, and I hope like hell she enjoys it.

9

———

SASHA

"*P*romise you're not mad about Ryder?" My gaze flickers to Brooke's reflection in the mirror as I apply the finishing touches to my makeup. Normally, I don't wear much but...

I want Easton to see me in a different light. I've added eye shadow, mascara, and a swipe of lipstick. Instead of wearing my hair in its usual ponytail, which is easier with soccer practice, I've left it to flow long and loose around my shoulders.

"Are you kidding?" She glances up from where she's lounging on my bed while painting her toenails with a metallic turquoise polish. "You might not realize this, but getting you together with Easton was the end goal all along."

My brows pinch together as I swing around to face her. "I'm sorry?"

With a careless shrug, she concentrates on lacquering her pinkie toe. "Yeah, I don't care how it happened, I'm just glad it finally did."

My mouth tumbles open. "But what about Ryder? I feel bad about how everything went down with him."

"Pfft. My cousin is just fine. I have my doubts that he's ready to settle down anyway." She shoots me a frown. "He enjoys the puck bunnies way too much to get into a relationship anytime soon."

This is…unbelievable.

I cock a hip before planting my fist on it. "What would have happened if I'd actually fallen for him?"

Brooke tilts her head and gives me a considering look. "Was there ever a remote possibility of that occurring? Like, I'm talking about a snowball's chance in hell kind of possibility."

Nope.

"That's not the point," I insist.

"Sure, it is. Plus, I'd never encourage you to get involved with a player. And Ryder is definitely a player. Just like Andrew." For a moment, her expression darkens and anger ignites in her eyes.

Even though Brooke is over her ex, she's been a little gun shy about getting involved with anyone else. I can't blame her for that. Andrew really screwed her over and the entire university knew about it, which only adds more salt to the wound. It's going to take time and the right guy to come along for her to even consider cracking open her heart again.

In the blink of an eye, she banishes the thunder clouds gathering on her pretty face. "You two just needed a push in the right direction, and I was all too happy to provide that nudge." She grins. "You're welcome."

The fears circling around in the back of my head escape before I can stop them. "What if it doesn't work out? What if we're better off as friends? What if we lack chemistry?" Even as I blurt out the last question, I know that won't be the case. The attraction between us—well, at least on my part—has been off the charts.

She rolls her eyes. "You worry too much, Sash. You've loved Easton for as long as you can remember."

When I open my mouth to protest, she cuts me off. "Don't bother denying it. I've watched you moon over the guy for years. It was painful."

"There hasn't been any mooning," I grumble, lying through my teeth.

"Yes, there was. No matter what, this needed to happen."

I press my lips together, unsure how to respond. Thankfully, the conversation is cut short when my phone chimes with an incoming message. My belly drops to the bottom of my toes, knowing that it can be none other than Easton. He's here and we're heading out for our first official date.

There's a part of me that can't believe this is actually happening. That he finally sees me in the same light I've always seen him.

Brooke glances up when I remain frozen in place. "Get going, girl!"

Her voice spurs me into action, and I swipe my black purse off the dresser before beelining for the door.

As I cross over the threshold into the hallway, she calls out my name. "Sash?" I swing back around. "Take a jacket and hat and have an amazing time with the guy of your dreams."

A small smile curls the edges of my lips as I suck in a deep breath before releasing it back into the atmosphere. "Thanks."

With a pounding heart, I race out of the apartment and down the stairwell to the lobby before pushing out into the darkness. I pause on the walkway before spotting Easton's truck idling in a parking space.

My hand flutters to my belly in an attempt to settle the butterflies that have winged their way to life. Even though I quickly sift through all of my memories, I know there's never been a time that I've been this nervous around him.

Whether I want it to or not, everything feels different now.

Our gazes meet across the lot and a sizzle of awareness scuttles down my spine as he lifts a hand to wave.

I return the gesture before hurrying to the passenger side, opening the door, and slipping inside. Barely do I open my mouth in greeting when his fingers slide through my hair to cup the side of my head before pulling me toward him until his mouth can settle over mine. That one touch is all it takes to lose myself on a rising tide of sensation. Just as I'm about to sink into the caress, he breaks away.

"Hey there."

"Hi." My voice comes out sounding breathy and high pitched, not at all like it usually does.

His lips curve into a slow smile as if he knows exactly how affected I am.

"You ready to do this?"

I jerk my head into a nod and attempt to put the kibosh on the chaos unfolding inside me.

"Glad to hear it." There's a pause and my breath catches, wondering if he's going to delve in for a second kiss. I'm disappointed when he doesn't.

"I think you're going to enjoy it."

It takes effort to dispel the haze clouding my mind. "You never mentioned what we're doing."

He sends me a cagey look before shifting the truck into reverse and backing out of the parking space. "Yup. That was purposeful."

I turn in my seat to face him as he pulls onto the street. "Wait a minute. Is it a secret?"

A smile simmers around the corners of his lips. "Maybe."

"Hmmm." I settle against the leather and stare out the windshield as my mind spins with all the possibilities. "Are you going to give me a clue?"

"Nope." Looking pleased with himself, he pops the P at the end of the word.

"Not even a little one?"

He presses his lips together before shaking his head.

I'd figured our date would be lowkey and we'd end up grabbing dinner somewhere and then hitting a party. Or maybe we'd see a movie. Something along those lines. But that obviously isn't part of the plan, since we're on the outskirts of town. The lights from the city fade before Easton turns onto a side road and we head into a county park. As we roll to a stop at a tiny, one-story building, he rolls down the window to speak with the guard.

"Hey, Mitch. How are you doing? Is everything set up?"

The blond guy grins as his gaze flickers to me. "Yup, all ready. Have fun."

"Thanks, take care," Easton says with a wave.

"You, too."

And then he's rolling up the window and we're driving on a narrow road that cuts through the woods.

He glances in my direction before focusing on the black ribbon of asphalt stretched out in front of us. "You want to take any guesses?"

I stare out at the vast darkness that surrounds us. "I have no idea what you're up to," I mutter, brows pinching together.

His grin widens. "Good, then it'll be a total surprise."

That it will.

After another five minutes of winding our way through trees that spear up into the night sky, the road opens into a wide parking lot. With the darkness blanketing us, it's difficult to figure out where we are or what we're even doing here. It takes a moment before my gaze sharpens on orange flames that dance and twist in the distance.

Is that a fire?

My attention slides to Easton in silent question. Instead of giving me an answer, he unleashes another smile before exiting the vehicle. And then he's jogging around the hood and opening the passenger side door.

When I don't move, he asks, "Do you trust me to give you an experience that you'll love?"

Of course I do.

"Yes."

"Then let's go."

He takes hold of my hand and pulls me from the truck. Once my feet touch the asphalt, he tugs me toward the wide swath of grass. Now that my eyes have adjusted to the darkness, I realize there's a lake in the distance and more trees that flank the shoreline. My gaze drifts to the fire again and the ring of large rocks that surrounds it. Two Adirondack chairs are parked near the small blaze and there's a red cooler next to them.

"I don't understand..."

"Remember all the times we went camping when we were kids?" He doesn't give me a chance to respond. "We would sit around the fire, cook hot dogs, and look at the stars, trying to find the Big Dipper. Then we'd roast marshmallows and make s'mores. You loved that so much."

A heavy wave of emotion crashes over me, threatening to suck me under as tears prick the backs of my eyes.

"I did. I loved all the trips we took when we were kids." Once we were in high school, it became more difficult to carve out time when our families weren't busy with work obligations and athletics.

I can't believe he remembered that.

Or even attempted to recreate it.

If I closed my eyes and inhaled the scent of burning wood and listened to the crickets chirping or the animals scurrying in the underbrush, I would be transported there again.

When I remain frozen in place, he says, "Here, sit down and let me get you something to drink." For the first time since he picked me up, uncertainty weaves its way through Easton's deep voice.

I settle on one of the wooden chairs as he pulls out a bottle of white wine from the cooler along with two plastic tumblers from a paper bag. He uncorks the wine and pours one cup before passing it to me. Mind still cartwheeling, I take a sip as he grabs a glass for himself. Once he's seated, he lifts his drink in the air.

"To old memories and making new ones."

We both take a sip as the quietness of the night settles around us. Even though there's a heightened level of tension swirling through the atmosphere, it's not one that's uncomfortable. It's more a feeling of anticipation.

There's a chill to the air and I'm glad Brooke suggested a hat and gloves. With the fire snapping and crackling a few feet away, I'm perfectly comfortable. My attention shifts from the fire to the handsome boy next to me. The one who has always been my best friend.

The one who now wants to be more.

Understanding dawns. "Did Brooke know about this?"

His lips lift into a smile. "I shot her a quick text before I picked you up."

That sneaky little bitch.

Before I can ask any more questions, he reaches out and takes hold of my fingers. A zip of electricity buzzes across my flesh. His gaze drops to our clasped hands as if he feels the burst of energy as well.

"Thank you for doing all this. The wine and the fire are amazing." No one has ever gone to such great lengths to make a date this special. No one but him could possibly know how much this means to me.

"Oh, you think this is it?" He shakes his head. "We're just getting started. I've got hot dogs in the cooler and everything we need to make s'mores."

My eyes widen. "Are you kidding?" I was content with the wine and peacefulness of the fire. This is the most relaxing evening I've spent in a long time. Add my favorite campfire foods from my childhood and I'm in heaven.

"Nope. Are you hungry? Want to roast some dogs?"

"Yes!" Now that he's talking about food, I'm starving.

Easton grabs the pack of hot dogs and I set my tumbler down before hunting for a couple of sticks. After a few minutes of searching, I find two branches that are strong and straight. He spears the dogs, and we place them near the flames. It doesn't take long before the skin is sizzling and they're perfectly golden.

I blow on mine to cool it off and nibble at one end.

Mmm.

So good.

We each devour two before Easton pulls out the marshmallows, graham crackers, and chocolate. We use the same sticks to stab the white sugary confection before holding them in the flames. Once the marshmallow turns golden brown, I pop it onto a cracker with a piece of chocolate until it resembles a sandwich before taking a bite. My eyelids feather closed as the sweet concoction explodes on my tongue. It takes me back to my childhood and fills me with happiness, which is exactly how I feel when I'm with Easton.

Between the two of us, we make about half a dozen s'mores. As I finish the gooey dessert, I smile at the guy next to me, feeling completely satisfied. When he asked me out on an official date, I wasn't sure how it would go, but it's turned out better than I could have ever imagined.

Easton leans toward me before stretching out his hand. "Come here. You've got a little something-something on your face."

Oh.

Well, that's embarrassing.

His thumb swipes across the corner of my mouth. My heart slams into my ribcage as he lifts his hand and brings it to his lips before sucking the digit into his mouth. His gaze stays locked on mine the entire time.

A groan rumbles up from his chest as he leans forward and scoops me out of the chair before depositing me on his lap. His arms slip around me as his mouth crashes onto mine. The moment his tongue sweeps over the seam of my lips, I open, allowing him entrance. The need to feel totally connected pulses through me as I pull him closer so that there isn't an inch of space between us.

If I was worried about the chemistry or thought the other night was a fluke, those fears are laid to rest. The energy we generate is combustible. It won't take much for it to explode. Every touch has it ratcheting up in intensity.

Just when I think I'll go up in a burst of flames, Easton pulls away. His breath comes out in short, sharp pants. His heavy-lidded gaze falls to my mouth before his tongue darts out to lick his lips as if he's able to taste me there.

"It might have taken me a while to realize that the girl I've always wanted was right in front of me, but I'm there now. And you're that girl, Sash. You always have been."

My heart melts at the sentiment.

It feels like I've been secretly waiting to hear those words forever.

And now here we are.

My hands slide upward until they can tangle in his short, mahogany-colored strands.

"You've always been it for me. And after a while, I didn't think it was possible for you to see me as anything other than a friend."

Our gazes stay locked as he rests his forehead against mine. "You've always been the most important person in my life. Maybe the kind of relationship we have is changing, but that never will."

"Promise?"

"Always."

10

EASTON

My arm is slung across Sasha's shoulders as we walk through the first floor of the house I share with four guys from the football team. With another playoff game victory under our belt, everyone is pumped and ready to party.

Having her tucked against my side feels more right than anything else ever has. It's as if everything has finally clicked into place. I could kick myself for being blind to the girl who has been a constant in my life since grade school. Who has stood by me every step of the way. Who, if I have my way, will continue to be there for years to come.

I understand her concerns about the two of us getting involved. She's the last person I want to lose. And since I don't have a crystal ball, there's nothing I can do to reassure her that won't happen. Although, if I were a betting man, I'd say that we have a pretty good chance of defying the odds. I already know and love everything about this girl. She's my world. Always has been. But the connection between us is deeper now. Stronger.

When Sasha tips her head and glances at me, everything inside my being stills. I just want to cup the sides of her face and kiss the hell out of her. Now that I've had a taste, I'm addicted to her sweetness.

Just as I'm about to do that, a voice interrupts, "Well, look at you two. Must have finally decided to make it official."

"Can't get any more official than this," I say as Crosby hoists a bottle of beer to his lips.

Unable to resist, I brush my mouth against hers. If we weren't in the middle of this crush, I'd take it further. But I want Sasha to be comfortable with the pace we've set. When she's ready for more, then that's exactly when it'll happen. For the time being, we're exploring and getting to know each other. And yeah, that includes a whole lot of foreplay.

Sasha strokes her fingers against my cheek, capturing my attention. "I see Brooke across the room. I'll be right back."

As she steps away, my fingers tighten around her wrist before tugging her to me for one more kiss. "Hurry back," I growl, hating the idea of her being out of my sight for long.

Color floods her cheeks. "I will."

And then she's gone, disappearing through the crowd. I can't help but track her movements as she reaches her friend.

"Jeez," Crosby grunts. "You really have it bad."

"Yup." There was a time when being so wrapped up in a girl would have embarrassed me, but that's no longer the case. With Sasha, everything is different.

I glance at my teammate, only to find him staring through the crowd at Sasha and Brooke.

Crosby can be a real moody SOB when he wants to be. Couple that with the lip ring, and the girls on campus go wild for him.

I'll be honest—I don't get it.

Since Sasha and I have always been friends, Crosby is cool with her. Although, I can't say the same for Brooke. Even when she was with Andrew, Crosby always seemed to have an issue with her. I'm not sure what the deal is. I guess with my teammate, he either likes you or he doesn't.

There's no in between. And for some odd reason, he doesn't care for her.

When she was dating Andrew, our teammate and Crosby's childhood friend, he avoided her like the plague. Now that they've broken up, he seems to go out of his way to poke and irritate her. It's not like she was the guilty party in that relationship. It was all Andrew.

What a dick.

When a guy throws his arm around Brooke and pulls her close, the expression on Crosby's face darkens.

I nod toward the girls. "You really don't like her. Why is that?"

Since Brooke and Sasha have roomed together for three years, I've known her just as long. I feel somewhat responsible for introducing her to Andrew.

His gaze flickers in my direction before arrowing to her again. "I don't have feelings about that girl one way or the other."

"Really? Could have fooled me."

Not bothering to respond, he lifts the bottle to his lips before downing the contents.

All right then...

When Sasha glances at me across the sea of people that separates us, our gazes lock and hold. She smiles and I can't help but return the easy expression.

"Everybody is getting wifed up around here," Crosby mutters. "It's fucking annoying."

"Actually, it's pretty great. Maybe you should give it a try some time."

He snorts. "No thanks. I'll stick with the easy pussy."

I clap him on the back before taking off. "Your loss."

"Hardly."

Not bothering to argue, I shake my head and blaze a path toward Sasha. Ten minutes was more than enough time without her. The moment I slip my arms around her body, everything once again feels right in the world.

I nuzzle her neck. "Tell me we don't have to stay long."

"We can leave whenever you're ready."

"Excellent." That's exactly what I wanted to hear. "Then let's get the hell out of here."

A gurgle of laughter escapes from her. "Really? This is your house. Your party. Aren't you responsible?"

"Nope." I glance around the ensuing chaos. "I have four roommates who can keep it under control." Or not.

"Want to go to my place?"

I hunker down just a bit in order to wrap one arm around the back of her knees and the other around her upper body before hoisting her against me. "I thought you'd never ask."

Sasha slips her arms around my neck as we head for the door.

There's only one place I want to be—and it's not here, partying with this bunch of assholes.

11

SASHA

*E*aston's lips are fused to mine as we crash through the apartment door and into the entryway. His hands are everywhere, touching and learning every part of me. Stroking over my body in ways I only imagined.

"I want you so bad, baby," he growls.

Barely can I catch my breath before his mouth crashes onto mine again. And then I'm lost on a sea of sensory overload. The way he kicks the door shut with his foot sends my belly into free fall. I've never seen Easton like this. So forceful and dominant. I love every bit of it.

He maneuvers us through the dining area and into the hallway until we find ourselves in my room.

His fingers drift to the hem of my shirt where they pause. He breaks away just enough to say, "As much as I want to be inside you, if you're not ready, then we'll wait. We won't do anything you're not comfortable with."

The thick length of his erection presses insistently against my belly.

"No, I'm ready. I want you. I want this." I don't think I've ever wanted anything more.

"Are you sure?" Before I can answer, he says, "Because I want you to be certain. No regrets."

"There won't be. I'm ready."

With that, I close the distance between us and press my lips against his. Before he can sink into the kiss, I pull away, retreating a step. Then another until his hands drop back to their sides. Confusion mingles with desire as he waits for my next move.

This time, it's my fingers that bite into the fabric of my shirt before lifting it over my head. It stays clutched in my hand for a heartbeat before I allow it to drop to the carpet. Then I reach around and unhook the clasp of my bra. As soon as it springs apart, the straps slide down my shoulders and arms, baring my breasts. My jeans get pushed down my thighs and kicked away until I'm standing before him in nothing more than my panties. His hot gaze licks over every inch of me, igniting a firestorm of need inside my core. I suck in a breath before hooking my thumbs beneath the thin waistband and rolling it down my hips until the lacy scrap of material is pooled around my ankles.

"You're so fucking beautiful," he groans.

It only takes two steps to swallow up the distance. My palms settle against his T-shirt-clad chest before drifting lower, gathering up the material and tugging it over his head until he's as bare-chested as I am.

My gaze follows the path of my hands trailing over sculpted muscle before flicking up to meet his. "I've always thought that you had an amazing body." It's a relief to finally tell him how I feel. To get it all out in the open. No more secrets.

My fingers glide to the button of his jeans, flicking it open and dragging down the zipper. And then my hand is delving inside his boxers to stroke over his thick erection. He groans when I tighten around him, pulling the hard length from the cotton fabric. As my thumb circles over the bulbous head, a bead of moisture gathers at the tip. I continue rubbing until more wells up before lifting the digit to my mouth and drawing it inside.

His eyes darken as he watches me.

"I've always wondered what you would taste like."

A groan escapes from him as I sink to my knees. My gaze stays pinned to his as I lean forward and press a kiss against him before my tongue darts out to trace over the blunt head. His fingers loosely tunnel through my hair before locking around my skull to hold me in place as I suck him into my mouth. As I slide up and down his cock, his hips gyrate until we fall into a steady rhythm. With every movement, I draw him in deeper until he's able to nudge the back of my throat.

"Mmm, if you keep that up, I'm gonna come."

The low rumble of his voice spurs me on. I want to give him more pleasure than any other girl ever has.

Just when his body stiffens, he gently pushes me away before sliding his arms around my upper body and hauling me to my feet. Then he presses a quick kiss against my lips.

"When I come, it's going to be inside your pussy. We'll save this," he nips at my lower lip before tugging it with his teeth, "for later."

"Are you sure?"

"Yup. I want to bury myself deep inside you."

A moment later, we're tumbling onto the bed. The material of his denim scrapes against the bare skin of my inner thighs as his weight settles on top of me. Our lips collide as his tongue delves inside my mouth.

"I should probably take these off," he murmurs.

"It might be helpful."

With a groan, he pushes away, coming to his feet before shoving the jeans and boxers down his thighs and tossing them aside. My gaze travels over the length of him. I wasn't lying when I said that Easton was gorgeous.

Broad shoulders, defined chest, tapered waist, and muscular thighs. Just looking at him is enough to have heat pooling between my legs and my heart fluttering with awareness.

He takes a step toward me before halting. "Condom."

I suck in a sharp lungful of air as he picks up his jeans and grabs a square foil packet from the back pocket. The mention of protection makes this all the more real.

"Are you having second thoughts?" He stills, gaze sharpening as if he's able to read my mind. "It's all right if you are."

His voice jolts me back to awareness, and I shake my head.

"No." I hold out my hand for him to take. "I'm ready for this."

He sets the condom on the bed before maneuvering between my thighs. His fingers stroke over me before zeroing in on my clit and caressing it with gentle circles.

"You like that, baby?"

My body shudders with pleasure and I'm barely able to groan out an answer. When I can't stand another moment of this sweet torture, he grabs the rubber and rips open the package before sliding it over his erection. Then he's resettling between my thighs.

His gaze drops to my core. "There's nothing more that I love than playing with you."

Carefully, he spreads my lips with his fingers. No one has ever stared at me with such intensity. Instead of being embarrassed by his perusal, it sends a fresh wave of arousal crashing over me. After he looks his fill, he crawls up my body until the blunt tip of his cock nudges my entrance. His elbows sink into the mattress as he holds himself up so that his full weight doesn't rest on me.

Our gazes lock as his warm breath feathers over my lips. When he presses forward, I widen my legs, wrapping them around his waist. Inch by inch, he sinks inside my heat, stretching me with his girth. There's a pinch of pain before it explodes into pleasure, ricocheting through my body.

Once he's buried to the hilt, he pauses, holding himself perfectly still as a look of concentration settles over his expression. It's as if he's doing his damnedest to beat back his baser impulses.

I lift my hand until it can drift across his shadowed jaw. "You don't need to hold back. I want it all. I want you to give me everything."

A groan rumbles up from his chest before exploding from his lips. "Are you sure? Once the restraint falls away, I won't be able to control myself. Your pussy feels too damn good. It's so tight, strangling the life out of my cock."

"You can let go."

That's all it takes for him to pull out of my body before driving inside again. His gaze stays locked on mine as he continues to thrust. It's only when stars explode behind my eyelids and I moan out my pleasure that he follows me headfirst over the edge. His muscles stiffen as he arches, throwing his head back. I open my eyes so that I can watch the intensity wash over him as he orgasms.

When every last drop has been wrung from his body, he collapses, burying his face in my hair until his warm breath can feather against my delicate flesh.

"You realize that I'm never going to let you go, right?"

My heart spasms in response. "I really hope you don't."

Not ever.

EPILOGUE

EASTON

 *wo years later...*

"HEY BABE, YOU READY TO GO?" My voice rings throughout the tiny apartment that Sasha and I have been renting for the last year.

"I'll be there in a minute. I'm just putting the finishing touches on my outfit."

I perk up at that bit of information. I'll take any opportunity to get my hands on that girl. "Do you need my special brand of assistance?"

That question is met with a loud snort of laughter. "Forget it! If that happens, we won't get out of here for another hour."

She's right about that. Although, I never hear her complaining about all the time I take in the bedroom. In fact, it's usually the opposite. Just as I decide to head into the room and lend a hand, Sasha walks out, looking like a million bucks.

A low whistle leaves my lips as my gaze travels down the length of her. "You look good enough to eat."

Speaking of eating...

"Don't get any ideas."

The girl knows me well.

"Where'd you get that dress? I don't remember seeing it before." And trust me, the way the silky black material clings to every dip and curve, I'd remember.

A smile lifts her lips as she does a little spin so I'm treated to the full effect.

Damn.

My gaze drops to her ass.

Already my cock is stirring.

What am I talking about?

I have a full-fledged boner going on right now.

The moment she meets my gaze, the expression on her face changes. Her eyebrows rise as she shakes her head before throwing out an arm to keep me at bay.

"No! We have reservations to meet Brooke and—"

"They can wait."

Slowly, she retreats. "Easton, I spent thirty minutes on my hair and makeup. You'll mess it all up!"

I shrug, not giving a damn. And once I'm deep inside her body, neither will she.

"I'll be careful," I cajole. "I won't even touch your hair. You can bend over the bed, and I can slap that perfect ass a few times."

Even though she's trying to keep her distance, heat leaps into her blue eyes, making them grow darker. It doesn't take much to get her going. It's just one of the things I love about her.

"You know that's the only way I'm going to make it through dinner without dragging you away from the table and fucking you in the bathroom."

Her breath catches at the reminder of what happened three months ago.

I tilt my head. "Or maybe that's what you want?"

A whimper escapes from her. I can almost see her mentally tumbling back in time and reliving the moment at the club where we'd been hanging out with friends.

When her back hits the wall, I stalk closer, caging her in before pressing my erection into the softness of her body and thrusting. "So, what's it gonna be, baby?"

Her forehead falls against my chest. "You're going to be my undoing, you know that?"

Yup, I do.

Because I feel the exact same way.

Maybe it took me a while to see what had always been right in front of me, but now that my eyes have been opened, I won't ever let her go.

She picks up her head until our gazes collide. "I love you."

I rub the tip of my nose against hers. "I love you, too. Always will. Now, get your ass in that room so I can have my wicked way with you."

She grins before doing exactly that.

The End

Want to read the next story in the Campus Series?
Campus God releases March 29th!
Pre-order here -) https://books2read.com/campusgod

Campus Player -) https://books2read.com/u/mYAxqV
Campus Heartthrob -) https://books2read.com/campusheartthrob
Campus Hottie -) https://books2read.com/campushottie

Join my newsletter for all the insider scoops -) https://www.subscribepage.com/l5v9e4

CAMPUS GOD

BROOKE

"Girl, I'm in desperate need of a break," my bestie says as we hustle our way through the crowd of students traveling across campus like a herd of slow-moving cattle.

"Easton wearing you out already with all that sex?"

Sasha's eyes widen as she knocks her shoulder into mine. "What? Of course not!"

I grin as her face turns beet red.

Uh-huh, sure…

I know *exactly* what's going on in the room across from mine. Those two are so loud it would be impossible *not* to know. Although, I can't begrudge Sasha for finding her happily ever after and enjoying every moment of it.

That girl deserves it.

She's been crushing on her best guy friend since they were kids and didn't think there'd come a time when Easton saw her as anything more than his soccer-playing gal pal. But dreams really do come true, because here we are. They've been going strong for about a month now.

And it's all thanks to yours truly. I'm the one who pushed her into going out with my hockey-playing cousin, Ryder. That was all the prompting Easton needed to see her for the gorgeous woman Sasha has grown into. And the rest is relationship history.

They fit so perfectly that it's almost like they've been together for years. Two pieces of the same puzzle.

Am I a wee bit jealous of what they have?

Of course not.

All right, maybe a little. Who wouldn't want to be with a guy who looks at you like you hung the moon in the sky especially for him? That's exactly the way it is with Easton.

My last relationship ended in spectacular disaster. We're talking flames, plumes of black smoke, and no survivors.

Andrew Hickenlooper.

Football player.

More like all-around player.

We were together for almost a year when I'd learned that he'd been cheating.

A nasty chlamydia diagnosis was the ultimate tip-off. Imagine sitting on a table in a doctor's office, only to be told you had an STI. And since I wasn't screwing around on the side, I knew exactly where it had come from.

The only thing worse than that was when he tried to deny it. When that didn't work, he'd attempted to tell me that I caught it from a toilet seat.

Ummm...no.

It's not called a sexually transmitted infection for nothing.

The situation jackhammered to an all-new low when I found out that almost everyone at Western knew he was screwing around behind my back, and that it had been going on throughout most of our relationship. I won't lie, for a few minutes, I'd considered transferring colleges.

But here's the thing—I didn't do anything wrong.

Even though it wasn't easy, I held my head up high and ignored all the ugly gossip until it eventually died down. Now, if Andrew would take a hint and leave me alone, I could finally put the whole nasty mess behind me, where it belongs.

"You might not have noticed, but the walls in our apartment are paper thin."

"Oh, god," she groans, cheeks growing more flushed with every step we take.

I can't resist the chuckle that slips free.

"If we could go to his place, I would. But you know what it's like over at the football house. Constant parties and cleat sniffers looking to get laid. I'd prefer to keep them away from my man."

"Like you have anything to worry about. That guy only has eyes for one girl and that's you, my friend."

It's sweet.

The smile that blooms across her face tells me that she knows it as well. Just as she opens her mouth to respond, strong arms wrap around her from behind and sweep her off her feet.

Literally.

Speak of the devil...

Sasha beams as Easton presses her against his muscular body. By the besotted look in my bestie's eyes, the world around her has completely fallen away. People jostle past, shooting irritated looks in their direction, but neither cares. It wouldn't surprise me to see little red and pink hearts dancing above their heads.

Ugh.

They're seriously too cute for words. It's enough to induce vomiting.

Just as I'm about to sigh, movement catches the corner of my eye. A shiver of awareness slices through me and the delicate hair at the nape of my neck prickles as my gaze lands on the figure loitering a few feet away.

Crosby Rhodes.

Left tackle for the Western Wildcats.

My initial reaction is to step away and put more distance between us, but I refuse to give him the satisfaction. Instead, I steel myself for a confrontation. I've spent too much time around him not to know exactly how this interaction will play out.

And that's badly.

The funny part—if there's anything amusing about this situation—is that he has a reputation on campus as a real player. The guy doesn't *do* girlfriends. To my knowledge, he's never entertained the idea of one. Even with his surly disposition, he can still charm the panties off any female within a ten-mile radius.

Except me.

To me, he's a total dickhead.

As soon as I make eye contact, his gaze drops, slowly crawling down the length of my body. Even though he's not physically touching me, that's exactly what his perusal feels like. It takes every ounce of self-control to remain motionless, so he doesn't see how much his scrutiny bothers me. Instead, I straighten my shoulders and grit my teeth before jutting out my chin in defiance. If he thinks he can burrow under my skin that easily, he's seriously mistaken.

By the time his onyx-colored depths return to mine, there's a slight curl to his upper lip and a dark look filling his eyes.

"Nice tits, McAdams. New push-up bra? They look bigger than usual. I like it."

"Fuck off, Rhodes." It takes effort to resist the urge to hunch over so that my breasts aren't as noticeable. Although, let's face it, when you wear a D cup, that's difficult to do. I've always been sensitive about the size of my boobs, and somehow, Crosby has figured it out.

He smirks as if pleased by my reaction. I have no idea what I did to provoke his ire, but it's been directed at me since Andrew first introduced us. If it had been possible to avoid the surly boy with the messy dark hair and lip ring, I would have done so after just one meeting. Unfortunately, that was impossible given that Andrew and Crosby are teammates, friends, and roommates. They share an apartment together off campus.

In the beginning, I went out of my way to be nice, figuring that with enough time and kindness, his attitude would thaw and he'd soften his stance. That never happened. If anything, his temperament grew nastier. Once it dawned on me that we were never going to sit around a campfire and sing Kumbaya, I avoided and ignored him.

Even though Andrew and I broke up six months ago, I still run into Crosby on campus and at parties. Sure, I could avoid the football players all together, but I refuse to give either of them that much power over my life. That being said, am I going to miss any of them, with the exception of Easton, when I graduate from Western in the spring?

Nope. Not even a little.

That's not to say they're all bad dudes. A couple of Sasha's soccer teammates are dating football players and they seem like nice guys. But after Andrew's total mindfuck, I have zero interest in getting wrapped up with another self-absorbed jock. There are too many girls at Western throwing themselves at their feet. Most of the ones who hooked up with Andrew knew he had a girlfriend and didn't give a crap.

So much for girl code.

After I dumped his ass, a good number of them came out of the woodwork to share all the gory details. Then they were all about pussy power and solidarity. Not so much when they were hoing around with my man behind my back.

"What?" He grins. "It was a compliment. You should take it that way."

"Please," I snort, "nothing that comes out of your mouth could be misconstrued as complimentary."

His smile widens, and the tiny silver hoop pierced through the corner of his lip glints in the sun. Without realizing it, my gaze drops to the metal. His tongue darts out to play with it, and a punch of arousal explodes in my core.

His voice dips as he looms closer. "Is that what you want, McAdams? My sweet words?" He practically purrs the question.

My heart kicks into overdrive as my attention snaps to his eyes. An unwanted sizzle of electricity snakes down my spine. One would think from our contentious past, the only thing he would do is piss me off.

Turns out that's not the case.

For whatever reason, Crosby is the only guy on this campus capable of making my hormones sit up and take notice. If there were away to stomp out the unwelcome attraction rushing through me like liquid fire, I'd do it in a heartbeat.

But there's not. Trust me, I've tried. Which is precisely why I go to such great lengths to avoid him. I would say like a clap diagnosis, but…

That hits a little too close to home.

I clear my throat. "Hardly."

He eats up more distance between us until it becomes necessary to tip my chin upward to hold his flinty gaze. It takes every ounce of self-control to stand my ground instead of scrambling backward in retreat.

The buzz of attraction zipping through my veins is not only disconcerting but refuses to be extinguished. His bright white teeth flash in the sunlight, and my attention is reluctantly snagged by the small metal hoop. I've never been attracted to guys with piercings. Or who are dark and moody.

Crosby is—and has always been—the exception to the rule.

When he reaches out to trail a finger down the front of my sweater, I jerk out of the strange stupor that has fallen over me and knock his hand away.

"Don't touch me," I growl, baring my teeth like a rabid dog. He's lucky I don't take a chunk out of him. At the very least, he'd think twice about messing with me in the future. Then again, nothing seems to deter him. He enjoys taunting me.

A slow grin spreads across his face as dark humor dances in his inky-colored irises.

Unwilling to get drawn into any more of a verbal skirmish, I spin on my heels and stalk through the crowd. Now that Easton has captured Sasha's attention, it's doubtful she'll notice my abrupt departure.

There's only so much of Crosby Rhodes I can take.

Want to read more of Brooke & Crosby's story? Buy it here -) https:// books2read.com/campusgod

HATE TO LOVE YOU

BRODY

"Dude, I thought you'd be back earlier." Cooper, one of my roommates, grins as I walk through the front door. There's a half-naked chick straddling his lap. "We had to get this party started without you." He shrugs as if he's just taken one for the team. "It couldn't be helped."

I snort as my gaze travels around the living room of the house we rent a few blocks off campus. Even though there are only four of us on the lease, our place seems to be a crash pad for half the team. By the looks of the beer bottles strewn around, they've been at it for a while. I'm seriously thinking about charging some of these assholes rent.

Although, I guess if I were stuck in a shoebox of a dorm, I'd be desperate for a way out, too. I played juniors straight out of high school for two years before coming in as a freshman at twenty. I skipped dorm living and went straight to renting a place nearby. There was no way I was bunking down with a bunch of random eighteen-year-olds who'd never lived away from home. Not to mention, having an RA up my ass telling me what I could and couldn't do.

That sounds about as much fun as ripping duct tape off my balls.

Which is, I might add, the complete opposite of fun. Hazing sucks.

And for future reference, you don't rip duct tape off your balls, you carefully cut it away with a steady hand while mother-fucking the entire team.

My other two roommates, Luke Anderson and Sawyer Stevens, are hunched at the edge of the couch, battling it out in an intense game of NHL. Their thumbs are jerking the controllers in lightning-quick movements, and their eyeballs are fastened to the seventy-inch HD screen hanging across the room.

I can only shake my head. Every time they play, it's like a freaking National Championship is at stake.

I arch a brow as the girl on Cooper's lap reaches around and unhooks her bra, dropping it to the floor. Apparently, she doesn't mind if there's an audience. Cooper's lazy grin stretches as his fingers zero in on her nips.

I'd love to say this scene isn't typical for a Sunday night, but I'd be lying through my teeth. Usually, it's much worse.

Deking out Luke with some impressive video game puck handling skills, Sawyer says, "Grab a beer, bro. You can take over for Luke after I make him cry again like a little bitch."

"Fuck you," Luke grumbles.

I glance at the score. Luke is getting his ass handed to him on a silver platter, and he knows it.

"Sure." Sawyer smirks. "Maybe later. But I should warn you, you're not really my type. I like a dude who's packing a little more meat than you."

My lips twitch as I drop my duffle to the floor.

"Hey, you see that bullshit text from Coach?" Cooper asks from between the girl's tits.

I groan, hoping I didn't miss anything important while I was out of town for the weekend. I'm already under contract with the Milwaukee Mavericks. My dad and I flew there to meet with the coaching staff. I also got to hang with a few of the defensive players. Saturday night was freaking crazy. Next season is going to rock.

"Nah, didn't see it," I say. "What's going on?"

"Practice times have changed," Cooper continues, all the while playing with the girl's body. "We're now at six o'clock in the morning and seven in the evening."

Fuck me. He's starting two-a-days already?

"You think he's just screwing around with us?" I wouldn't put it past Coach Lang. I don't think he has anything better to do than lie awake at night, dreaming up new ways to torture us. The guy is a real hard-ass.

Then again, that's why we're here.

But six in the morning...that sucks. Between school and hockey practice, I already feel like I don't get enough sleep. And it's only September. That means I'll need to be up and out the door by five to make it to the rink, get dressed, and be on the ice by six. By the time eleven o'clock at night rolls around, I'll fall into bed an exhausted heap.

Sawyer shrugs, not looking particularly put out by the time change.

Cooper pops the nipple out of his mouth and fixes his glassy-eyed gaze on me. "Can't you have your dad talk some freaking sense into the guy?"

Luke grumbles under his breath, "I can barely make it to the seven o'clock practice on time."

"Nope." I shake my head. I'd do just about anything for these guys, except run to my father with anything related to hockey. Coach and my dad go way back. They both played for the Detroit Redwings. I've known the man my entire life. He helped me lace up my first pair of Bauers. So, you'd think he'd have a soft spot for me. Maybe take it easy on me.

Yeah...fat chance of that happening.

If anything, he comes down on me like a ton of bricks *because* of our personal relationship. I think Lang doesn't want any of the guys to feel like he's playing favorites.

Mission accomplished, dude.

No one would ever accuse him of that.

"Then prepare to haul ass at the butt crack of dawn, my friend."

With that, Cooper turns his attention elsewhere, attacking the girl's mouth.

Luke eyes them for a moment before yelling, "Hey, you gonna take that shit to the bedroom or are we all being treated to a free show?"

Not bothering to come up for air, Cooper ignores the question.

Luke shakes his head and focuses his attention on making a comeback. Or at least knocking Sawyer's avatar on its ass. "Guess that means we should make some popcorn."

I pick up my duffel and hoist it over my shoulder, deciding to head upstairs for a while. I love hanging with these guys, but I'm not feeling it at the moment.

"Hi, Brody." A lush blonde slips her arms around me and presses her ample cleavage against my chest. "I was hoping you'd show up."

Given the fact that this is my house, the chances of that happening were extremely high.

I stare down into her big green eyes.

"Hey." She looks familiar. I do a quick mental search, trying to produce a name, but only come up with blanks.

Which probably means I haven't slept with her recently.

When it comes to the ladies, I've come up with an algorithm that I've perfected over the last three years. It's simple, yet foolproof. I never screw the same girl more than three times in a six-month period. If you do, you run the risk of entering into the murky territory of a quasi-relationship or a friends-with-benefits situation. I'm not looking for any attachments at this point.

Even casual ones.

I'm at Whitmore to earn a degree and prepare for the pros. I'm focused on getting bigger, faster, and stronger. The NHL is no place for pussies. If you can't hack it, the league will chew you up and spit you out before you can blink your eyes. I have no intention of allowing that to happen. I've worked too hard to crash and burn at this point.

Or get distracted.

In a surprisingly bold move, Blondie slides her hand from my chest to my package and gives it a firm squeeze to let me know she means business.

I have no doubts that if I asked her to drop to her knees and suck me off in front of all these people, she would do it in a heartbeat. Other than a thong, the girl grinding away on Cooper's lap is naked.

My first year playing juniors, when a girl offered to have no-strings-attached-sex, I'd thought I'd hit the flipping jackpot. Less than five minutes later, I'd blown my load and was ready for round two. Fast forward five years, and I don't even blink at a chick who's willing to drop her panties within minutes of me walking through the door. It happens far too often for it to be considered a novelty.

Which is just plain sad.

When I was in high school, I jumped at the chance to dip my wick.

Now?

Not so much.

It's like being fed a steady diet of steak and lobster. Sure, it's delicious the first couple of days. Maybe even a full week. You can't help but greedily devour every single bite and then lick your fingertips afterward. But, believe it or not, even steak and lobster become mundane.

Most guys, no matter what their age, would give their left nut to be in my skates.

To have their pick of any girl. Or, more often than not, *girls*.

And here I am...limp dick in hand.

Actually, limp dick in *her* hand.

Sex has become something I do to take the edge off when I'm feeling stressed. It's my version of a relaxation technique. For fuck's sake, I'm twenty-three years old. I'm in the sexual prime of my life. I should be ecstatic when any girl wants to spread her legs for me. What I shouldn't be is bored. And I sure as hell shouldn't be mentally running through the drills we'll be doing when I lead a captain's practice.

I pry her fingers from my junk and shake my head. "Sorry, I've got some shit to take care of."

And that shit would be school. I have forty pages of reading that needs to be finished up by tomorrow morning.

Blondie pouts and bats her mascara-laden lashes.

"Maybe later?" she coos in a baby voice.

Fuck. That is such a turnoff.

Why do chicks do that?

No, seriously. It's a legitimate question. Why do they do that? It's like nails on a chalkboard. I'm tempted to answer back in a ridiculous, lispy-sounding voice.

But I don't.

I'm not that big of an asshole.

Plus, she might be into it.

Then I'd be screwed. I envision us cooing at each other in baby voices for the rest of the night and almost shudder.

"Maybe," I say noncommittally. Although I'm not going to lie, that toddler voice has killed any chance for a later hookup. But I'm smart enough not to tell her that. Chances are high that she'll end up finding another hockey player to latch on to and forget all about me. Because let's face it, that's what she's here for.

A little dick from a guy who skates with a stick.

Just to be sure, I run my eyes over the length of her again.

Toddler voice aside, she's got it going on.

And yet, that banging body is doing absolutely nothing for me.

Which is troublesome. I almost want to take her upstairs just to prove to myself that everything is in proper working order. But I won't.

As I hit the first step, Cooper breaks away from his girl. "WTF, McKinnon? Where you going?" He waves a hand around the room. "Can't you see we're in the middle of entertaining?"

"I'll leave you to take care of our guests," I say, trudging up the staircase.

"Well, if you insist," he slurs happily.

My bedroom is at the end of the hall, away from the noise of the first floor. As a general rule, no one is allowed on the second floor except for the guys who live here. I pull out my key and unlock the door before stepping inside.

My duffel gets tossed in the corner before I open my Managerial Finance book. I thought I'd have a chance to plow through some of the reading over the weekend, but my dad and I were on the go the entire time. Meeting people from the Milwaukee organization, hitting a team party, checking out a few condos near the lakefront. Just getting the general lay of the land. On the plane ride home, I had every intention of being productive, but ended up sacking out once we hit cruising altitude.

Three hours later, there's a knock on the door. Normally an interruption would piss me off, but after slogging through thirty pages, my eyes have glazed over, and I'm fighting to stay awake. This material is mind-numbingly boring, and that's not helping matters.

"It's open," I call out, expecting Cooper to try cajoling me back downstairs.

When that guy's shitfaced, he wants everyone else to be just as hammered as he is. I've never seen anyone put away alcohol the way he does. It's almost as impressive as it is scary. And yet, he's somehow able to wake up for morning practice bright-eyed and bushy-tailed like he wasn't just wasted six hours ago. Someone from the biology department really needs to do a case study on him, 'cause that shit just ain't normal.

When I suck down alcohol like that, the next morning I'm like a newborn colt on the ice who can't keep his legs under him.

It's not a pretty sight. Which is why I don't do it. Been there, done that. Moving on.

The door swings open to reveal Blondie-With-The-Toddler-Voice. And she's not alone. She's brought a friend.

I raise my brows in interest as they step inside the room.

In the three hours since I've seen her, Blondie has managed to lose most of her clothing. The brunette she's with appears to be in the same predicament. They stand in lacy bras and barely-there thongs with their hands entwined.

My gaze roves over them appreciatively.

How could it not?

Their tummies are flat and toned. Hips are nicely rounded. Tits jiggle enticingly as they saunter toward the bed where I'm currently sprawled.

I should be a man of steel over here. I haven't gotten laid in three weeks. Which is almost unheard of. I haven't gone that long without sex since I first started having it.

But there's nothing.

Not even a twitch.

Which begs the question—What the hell is wrong with me?

It must be the stress of school and the skating regimen I'm on. Even though I'm already under contract with Milwaukee and don't have to worry about the NHL draft later this year, I'm still under a lot of pressure to perform this season.

National Championships don't bring themselves home.

I'd be concerned that I have some serious erectile dysfunction issues happening except there's one chick who gets me hard every time I lay eyes on her. Rather ironically, she wants nothing to do with me. I think she'd claw my eyes out if I laid one solitary finger on her.

Actually, all I have to do is stare in her direction, and she bares her teeth at me.

Maybe these girls are exactly what I need to relieve some of my pent-up stress. It certainly can't hurt.

Decision made, I slam my finance book closed and toss it to the floor where it lands with a loud thud. I fold my arms behind my head and smile at the girls in silent invitation.

And the rest, shall we say, is history.

Want to read more of Brody and Natalie's story?
You can buy it here -) https://books2read.com/u/bPXN6x

ABOUT THE AUTHOR

Jennifer Sucevic is a USA Today bestselling author who has published twenty New Adult novels. Her work has been translated into German, Dutch, and Italian. Jen has a bachelor's degree in History and a master's degree in Educational Psychology. Both are from the University of Wisconsin-Milwaukee. She started out her career as a high school counselor, which she loved. She lives in the Midwest with her husband, four kids, and a menagerie of animals. If you would like to receive regular updates regarding new releases, please subscribe to her newsletter here- Jennifer Sucevic Newsletter (subscribepage.com) Or contact Jen through email, at her website, or on Facebook.

sucevicjennifer@gmail.com

Want to join her reader group? Do it here -)

J Sucevic's Book Boyfriends | Facebook

Social media links-

https://www.tiktok.com/@jennifersucevicauthor

www.jennifersucevic.com

https://www.instagram.com/jennifersucevicauthor

https://www.facebook.com/jennifer.sucevic

Amazon.com: Jennifer Sucevic: Books, Biography, Blog, Audiobooks, Kindle

Jennifer Sucevic Books - BookBub